Andrew Ranson: St. Augustine's Pirate

A Historical Novel of 17th-Century Intrigue

K. Ross Lee
and
Betsy S. Lee

ISBN-13: 978-0692339480

Cover design Betsy S. Lee

Published by:
K B Aren LLC
www.kbaren.com

CONTENTS

Acknowledgments i

1. November 1684 Andrew Ranson – St. Augustine, Florida 1

2. 1649 England and Spanish Jamaica 5

3. 1650, England The Duke and Duchess of Newcastle-upon-Tyne 7

4. 1657 Mr. Wormer 14

5. 1666–1668 The Farm 22

6. 1670 The *Cagway* 29

7. 1670–1671 Lady Elizabeth Loxley 37

8. 1668–1672 A New Life 43

9. 1675 Abigail's Birthday 49

10. Life at Sea 60

11. 1679 The Dinner 66

12. The Investigation 74

13 . The Ring 78

14. Jumping Ship 82

15. The Voyage 88

16. Rescue at Sea 93

17. The Discovery 95

18. The Grand Plan 99

19. Man-O'-War 108

20. Queen Anne's War 111

Glossary 113

References 115

Dictionaries 119

Authors' Note 121

About the Authors 123

ACKNOWLEDGMENTS

The authors wish to thank the following organizations (listed in no particular order) for their cooperation in our endeavors to secure the historical facts that established Florida in the New World: Castillo de San Marcos, Fort Caroline, and The Florida Historical Association.

Thank you to the members of the Florida Writers Association and the Professional Writers Group for their input and support.

In no particular order, the authors are especially grateful to: Beth Mansbridge, for her extraordinary copyediting abilities and her professionalism and friendship; Aileen Quinn Wietstruk, for her friendship, insight of 17th-century lifestyles, and for helping us expand the book; Kareen Saum, for her patience in helping to develop the book; and to Bob and Ruth Feldheim, for their encouragement and advice. To Dr. Dorothy Headley Israel and Edy Luke, for our wonderful breakfast meetings on Thursday mornings, and for suffering through our sometimes too loud debates, and their invaluable input and encouragement that we see this book to completion.

Chapter 1

November 1684
Andrew Ranson – St. Augustine, Florida

Andrew Ranson languished in a dank cell of the partially completed Castillo de San Marcos, awaiting his fate. His torn shirt exposed festering welts from lashes of a whip that had dug deep into his back, leaving a strange pattern across his broad, muscular shoulders. He sat hunched over on a pile of moldy straw, holding his head, trying to contain the pain. A narrow stream of light snaked from under the huge door, but did not relieve either the wrenching sting in his head or the desolation of his surroundings.

The heavy door creaked open. Andrew's heart pounded when he looked up and saw the silhouette of a huge, double-chinned, pot-bellied priest.

Mechanically, the priest outstretched his hands into the foul air, closed his eyes, and uttered, "My son, you must now confess your sins before God, and repent."

From his robe, he pulled out a cloth and spread it on the filthy ground. With great effort, he knelt before Andrew.

Leaning forward, he placed a hand on Andrew's matted hair and said, "Let us pray."

"Father … I have nothing to confess." Andrew's words sounded labored and bitter. Tears ran down his face. "I'm innocent," he said, lowering his voice a pitch. "They tortured me into confessing I was a pirate."

The priest quickly removed his hand and began again. "My son, if you are truly innocent, God would have given you the courage and strength to endure the torture. Let us pray and celebrate the Eucharist together."

Andrew's thoughts spiraled. He uttered, "Father, I'm not sure I believe in God or Jesus."

The priest huffed. "Andrew," he said, "I must administer the sacrament of the Viaticum now!"

"What is that?"

"Did you learn nothing about religion?" Before Andrew could answer, the priest snapped, "It is Latin for 'provisions for a journey.' Now let us pray." All the while he was thinking, *How can I, a man of the cloth, in good conscience administer the last rites to this Andrew Ranson when he doubts the existence of God?*

From the first line of his recitation of the Viaticum, the priest's sorrowful voice reverberated off the coquina walls. Andrew's fear increased tenfold upon hearing faint footsteps. The sound intensified. Andrew's eyes twitched, his mouth became cotton-dry. The priest continued praying as twelve formidable guards halted at attention in the doorway.

"It's time, let's go!" came a callous bellow.

Terrified and struggling to his feet, Andrew broke out in a cold sweat.

A guard grabbed Andrew's hands and tied his wrists in front of him. Andrew's knees buckled and another guard caught him.

With tremendous effort, the priest pushed his own great bulk up. Short of breath, he chanted prayers in Latin, and Andrew's gaze followed him making his way to the front of the guards' formation. The priest continued to chant Latin prayers while leading the way to the plaza.

Staggering between the guards, Andrew, unmindful of the nearby glittering Matanzas Bay or the murmurings of the throng, was only aware of the blazing sun on his slumped shoulders and head. He felt ready to fall to the ground.

The priest, guards, and Andrew seemed to proceed in slow motion ... approaching a grove of trees where a raised platform stood before the crowd. There the executioner and the garrote stood facing the assembled soldiers from the presidio, Franciscan friars, and the newly appointed governor, Juan Marquez Cabrera. Two guards stepped out of formation, and pushed and pulled Andrew up the stairs, onto the platform. The executioner moved a step closer to the garrote, an upright palm log with a hole drilled neck high. He threaded a rope through the hole, wound it around Andrew's neck and back through the hole, and then tied the two ends to a stout stick.

Governor Cabrera stepped onto the platform, turned to Andrew Ranson, and read the death warrant in a loud voice. The crowd quieted only after the governor stopped speaking. He nodded to the priest and left.

Father Perez de la Mota, of the Castillo and the commission of the inquisition, turned to the prisoner and asked, "Andrew, do you have any last words?"

Tears streamed down Andrew's face. In a barely audible voice, he said, "Rosary, my mother's rosary." He sighed. "Please put it in my hands."

Andrew closed his eyes. The priest lifted the rosary from Andrew's neck and placed it into his bloodstained hands. The doomed man clasped the worn beads; the small silver cross slipped down between his fingers.

Though strident cries now came from the mob, Andrew felt engulfed in silence while the friars chanted their prayers.

A hush came over the crowd when the enormous man in the black hood stepped closer to the back of the garrote and began slowly twisting the stick. One turn and the rope tightened snug to Andrew's neck. The second turn ... the prisoner gasped ... the third turn ... the rope bit into

Andrew's neck and blood trickled from his throat. Andrew struggled to breathe against the tightness. A fourth turn … a fifth, and his eyes bulged … a sixth turn of the stick … the executioner started giving the stick one more mighty turn. Andrew's face turned a purplish-blue color. His body twisted, jerked, and slumped.

Church bells started their toll for Andrew's departed soul. However, on the last twist, the rope snapped and broke in two. Andrew fell forward like a rag doll onto the wooden platform, panting.

Stunned, Father Perez de la Mota raised an arm toward the heavens, with Bible in hand, and cried out, "It's a miracle! Andrew Ranson has been saved by God!"

The crowd gasped in unison.

Father Carlos, who had led Andrew to the Plaza de la Constitucion, thought, *This is proof there exists a God.*

The Franciscan friars lifted Andrew's limp body.

Father Perez de la Mota commanded, "Take him to the church. I give this man sanctuary! Let no man harm him, or they will suffer the wrath of God."

Governor Cabrera yelled out, "No! Garrote him again!"

Chapter 2

1649
England and Spanish Jamaica

Ranie's lighter skin had its rewards in Jamaica. It meant she did not have to toil in the fields like some of her darker friends. She derived satisfaction in her role of supervisor at the large Spanish plantation.

The staff loved and respected her. They confided their hopes and dreams, and disclosed what they overheard.

"An English duke goin' buy the plantation."

"No!" Ranie answered.

"It's the truth, I tell you. Not only that, the master and his entire family are mov'n to St. Augustine, La Florida."

Ranie reassured them, "It's hearsay" … until a few months later when Eli, a handsome, bilingual, retired officer of the English Horse Guards arrived, representing the Duke of Newcastle-upon-Tyne, to inspect the plantation. His orders were, upon completion, to bring back samples of the plantation produce for the duke to inspect.

Eli stayed six months and, smitten by Ranie, spent considerable time with her. He taught her some English. When she announced to Eli that she was pregnant with his child, he was thrilled and wanted her to return to England with him in hopes she would deliver him a son.

The only home she knew was the plantation and she did not want to leave. However, Eli promised her a good life. His loving ways convinced her.

†††

Shortly after arriving in England, she gave birth to a sickly child. Eli now showed another side of himself that she never seen. Eli blamed Ranie for the baby's ill health. She was devastated when he abandoned them.

The Duchess of Newcastle-upon-Tyne, now eight and a half months along in her own pregnancy, felt partly responsible for Eli's reprehensible act.

After summoning Ranie, the duchess explained, "God sent you to be my baby's wet nurse."

Though taken aback at this pronouncement, Ranie recovered and accepted the offer gratefully. Employed again, she no longer worried about being able to care for her sick baby.

Chapter 3

1650, England
The Duke and Duchess of Newcastle-upon-Tyne

The sun's rays pierced through the canopy of old English oaks that lined either side of the earthen road and illuminated the ornate polished gate and family crest of the Duke and Duchess of Newcastle-upon-Tyne. Sprawling manicured grounds lay beyond the gate. Formal, geometrically shaped boxwoods stood like guards at attention along the wide, straight approach to the manor.

A seldom-used room in the manor had been prepared for the birth. The velvet drapes, hanging partially closed, were as red as the blood issuing from the duchess.

Ranie and several other servants stood stoically around the room waiting for instructions, as the duchess screamed out the excruciating pain of her premature labor.

Dr. Wallingford and Dr. Bassill tried to stop her bleeding. Dr. Austin stood at the head of the bed. He held the duchess's shoulders in a forceful manner while she thrashed and cried out.

Nodding to Ranie, Dr. Wallingford said, "Another towel quickly, please."

Ranie reached for a towel from a ready pile and held it out to the handsome Dr. Wallingford. He peered at her light-umber skin and started to say something, but caught himself and merely took the towel out of Ranie's hand.

Ranie's eyes narrowed. She wanted to respond but remained silent, thinking, *Damn white men!* Ranie instantly chastised herself for being lost in thought at such a moment.

Wiping his hands, he remarked to his colleagues, "She experienced no problems with her two other pregnancies."

Hysterically, the duchess yelled at the same moment Dr. Bassill announced, "The head is crowning!"

Drenched in sweat, the duchess moaned and screamed.

Dr. Austin placed his hand on her forehead and said, "She has a high fever."

Fearing the worst, Dr. Wallingford sadly responded, "It's probably an infection. We must tell the duke of the life-threatening situation his wife is in."

✝✝✝

Down the corridor, the duke waited impatiently in his library. Dark wooden panels encased the room where he often sought refuge. Light streaming in through two windows reflected onto the decorated white plaster ceiling, which brightened the room somewhat. The family coat of arms, a shield with a four-masted ship surrounded by Tudor roses, was prominently displayed above the fireplace.

Trying to distract himself from the forthcoming birth of his third child, Edward picked up his most prized book, the Johannes Gutenberg Bible printed in 1450. Clutching the book to his chest, he brought it to his desk, sat down, and carefully opened the Bible to the verse of Matthew 6:27. He read: *Which of you by being anxious can add a single cubit to his life's span?* However, this did not distract him. Thinking, *It's been hours. My other children were born in a timely manner,* he felt a new emotion— vulnerability. He thought feeling anxious was bad enough, but helplessness was unfamiliar.

More hours dragged on. His mind wandered. He stared blankly at the pages.

Finally, a knock on the huge wooden pocket door roused him.

"Come in."

The servant laboriously slid the door open and announced, "Sir, congratulations, you have a new son."

The duke closed the Bible, stood up, and asked, "Are they all right?"

The servant lowered his head and said, "D-Dr. W-Wallingford … wants …"

"Speak up, Henry."

"He … wants to speak to you … before you see the duchess."

A cold sweat dampened the duke's body, his legs turning to jelly, and his mind raced: *Why would he want to see me?*

†††

Head erect and shoulders squared, the duke walked at a measured pace down the long, portrait-decorated corridor. His heart pounding harder with every step, he felt the eyes of his ancestors following him.

Dr. Wallingford stood waiting outside the duchess's door when the duke approached him.

Wallingford extended his hand and said, "Congratulations, Edward, my old friend, the baby is a healthy boy."

The duke smiled.

The doctor peered into the duke's all-observing, sunken eyes, trying to gauge him. "However, the duchess is at risk; she lost too much blood. We do not expect her to survive more than a few hours."

The duke's hands shook uncontrollably. Horrified, he thundered, "You must save her!"

"We've done everything we know to do. Now, go to your wife and child, they need you."

This cannot be happening, Edward thought.

The doctor opened the door and stepped aside for his friend to enter the birthing room. The duke's eyes widened when he saw the duchess, whose once rosy and luminescent porcelain skin was now sallow. He rushed to her bedside. She lay propped up on three feather pillows, looking spent. However, his newborn son, with the pink face of a cherub, lifted the father's spirits.

The corners of the duchess's lips curved up like a crescent moon while cradling her new son. The duke sensed a feeling of completion about her.

Tears ran down her cheeks. In a barely audible voice she said, "Look, Edward." She paused, and with great effort, continued. "A healthy, beautiful baby boy. He even bears your family's birthmark."

The infant cooed. His tiny hands made their way up through the swaddling and touched her tears.

Forcing a smile, the duke said, "Yes, my love, he is beautiful." Meanwhile he thought, *You have drained my beloved of all.*

Trying to stay composed, he cupped his hand on the baby's head and asked, "What did you decide to name him?"

"I want to call him Andrew, after my dear departed brother."

The duke bent down, kissed his wife on her forehead, and announced, "Andrew will be his name—"

"I know I will not be here to bring him up," she said in a muted voice while the tears streaming down her face dampened the pillow. "Please promise me you will provide for him."

"You mustn't say that! You now have three children to nurture."

She ignored his comment and, with labored breath, whispered, "My rosary, please give it to me."

Ranie, standing next to the bedside table where the rosary lay, picked it up.

The duchess said, "Please put it around Andrew's neck."

With great care, Ranie slid the rosary over the baby's head. She stepped back. The priest went over and gave the duchess her last rites.

The duchess, while cradling the infant in one arm, gestured for the duke to come closer. He put his ear to his wife's lips.

"Take care of him," she whispered, and then exhaled her last breath.

Ranie instinctively picked up the baby and tried to transfer Andrew to the duke, but he turned away, saying, "Get that murderer out of my sight. I never want to see it again!"

The duke knelt beside the bed, clutched the duchess's hand, and kissed it. He prostrated himself over her dead body and wailed.

†††

Two weeks after the death of his wife, the duke sent for Ranie.

She entered the room with Andrew cradled in her arms and, while trying to hand him his son, said, "Sir, Andrew is a healthy boy."

The duke turned his head and put his palms up as a barrier. "Take it away! Now!"

Profoundly upset, she thought of her own sickly baby. Thoughts whirled through her head: *How could he do this? His own flesh and blood!*

Ranie nodded to a nearby servant, placed Andrew into his arms, and signaled for him to leave.

Her heart heavy, she asked, "Sir, how can I be of service?"

The duke stared at the floor as he proclaimed, "I promised the duchess I would provide for it." He looked up and sighed. "In memory of my dear wife, I will live up to my word. However, I never want to see or speak of it again. You will take it back to your homeland in Jamaica, to raise as your own."

The duke went to his elaborate desk and sat in the chair behind it.

Making eye contact with Ranie, he said, "It is never to know of its heritage."

Ranie's mind raced: *I'm to raise him as my own!* She stood silent while her emotions went into a panicked state. *How will I take care of two children?*

The duke unlocked a drawer and removed a large envelope. "Here are enough English pounds to give Andrew a decent education and cover additional expenses. I instructed my solicitors to send you an annual stipend until he reaches manhood. Furthermore, I have booked passage on the *Jamaica Merchant*. It sails from Dover on the twentieth. My carriage will transport you and *it* to meet the ship. Never speak of his true family. Now get *it* out of my home and England!"

†††

Boarding the ship with careful steps, she held Andrew, who lay quietly in one of her arms, while her own child cried uncontrollably.

A week out from land, they encountered a wind which pushed the ship faster than expected. One night, thunderheads poured rain in sheets. The sky lit up and the next moment everything turned black. The storm was so loud it made Ranie's skin crawl.

Ranie thought, *We're never going to make it.*

Andrew slept in his basket while she held her own child tightly to her chest. His skin felt on fire. Trying to soothe her infant, tears ran down her cheeks. By the time the storm had passed over, her child lay dead in her arms.

Later, the captain gently lifted the child from her arms, said a prayer, and committed the tiny body to the sea.

Even in her grief, Ranie thought, *God has given me another son.*

Chapter 4

1657
Mr. Wormer

With the funds received from the duke and his solicitors, Ranie purchased a small farm near Port Royal. She planted crops of sugarcane and rice, which flourished. Later she expanded her farm and grew tobacco.

Over the years, the townspeople continued to talk about Ranie's success and the little white boy who called her "Mother."

Andrew's dark-brown hair streaked with golden highlights constantly fell over his intensely luminous chestnut-brown eyes. He tirelessly worked by his mother's side, tilling the land, never revealing his loathing for farming. Short for his age, high-spirited and smart, with a warm personality, he loved to go into town with Ranie because she took him to the docks to watch the tall ships.

†††

One day after dinner, Ranie decided it was time to tell Andrew her ambitions for him. "My son, I taught you all I know. You're smart and the world's big. I hope someday you may become a physician or a solicitor and live in a big house."

I don't want to live in a big house. I want to be a sailor and live on a ship, he thought.

Ranie went on: "It will require you to learn many things."

"Mother, I know a lot already."

"Yes, but there many more things you must learn. …"

†††

Anticipating his seventh birthday, Andrew chuckled and said, "Tomorrow is you know what!"

Ranie giggled and teased back. "What are you talking about, my dear child?"

Andrew scrunched his face and put his hands on his hips. "My seventh birthday!"

"Hmm …" Ranie put her finger to her temple. "Is it, now?" Staring into his eyes she declared, "I forgot—of course, dear—it's your birthday." She laughed and gave him a kiss on the forehead. "Now go to bed. Tomorrow I'll have a surprise for you."

"Oh, Mother, what did you get me?" Andrew's face softened.

"You'll see, now go to bed."

Morning couldn't come fast enough for Andrew. He was still putting on his shirt as he rushed into the kitchen. Ranie smiled to herself while he plopped down on the kitchen chair.

"Andrew, my son, I've hired a tutor to further your education."

"Oh! But what am I getting for my birthday, Mother?"

"A tutor."

"A tutor? That's my present?"

"Your future is your present."

†††

Yellow passionflowers entwined tightly on the white picket fence which surrounded their farmhouse, where

15

Ranie and Andrew stood waiting for his tutor. Feeling the sun heating her face, Ranie closed her eyes and inhaled the sweet scent of the tropical flowers. Andrew, on the other hand, was impatient. He kept jiggling his foot, and crossing and uncrossing his arms.

It wasn't long before they heard the clip-clop of approaching hooves. Two horses with heads and tails held high neighed as they pulled the carriage.

The driver yelled, "Whoa!"

The horses kicked the dirt up as they came to a stop.

A dignified, tall, thin man with long saffron-colored hair emerged from the carriage, dressed in a white ruffled shirt, black pants, and an open short waistcoat.

Ranie whispered, "My son, Mr. Wormer, your tutor, is here."

Mr. Wormer walked over to them. Ranie extended her hand and he politely kissed it. She grinned.

Perplexed, Andrew thought, *Why do I need him? He has a kind face. Maybe he brought me a present.*

Mr. Wormer shook Andrew's hand and said, "It's a pleasure to meet you, Master Andrew."

Andrew smirked, folded his arms across his chest, and brazenly said, "I don't need a tutor. I'm seven now and can read, count, and print my words."

Embarrassed, Ranie put her hand on Andrew's shoulder and gently squeezed it. "My son, you don't understand, but someday—"

The boy pulled away.

Mr. Wormer's many years as a tutor to young lads let him feel at ease in what otherwise could have been an awkward situation, and thus Mr. Wormer managed a smile.

Ranie spontaneously went on. "Mr. Wormer will teach you many things."

"I know a lot of things, Mother."

She put an arm around him. "Son, you'll learn higher mathematics, geography, history, proper English, Spanish,

Dutch, and French. And you'll learn how to read the stars and use an astrolabe."

"Why do I need to learn all that?"

"You'll be able to venture anywhere and never get lost."

His shoulders slumped and he kicked the dirt. "But Mother—"

"Hush now. Tomorrow he will bring his things and live in the back room, my son."

Andrew muttered under his breath, "He talks funny."

Ranie's expression tightened, and using a carefully controlled tone she said, "Mr. Wormer is a Dutchman and was educated in Holland."

Befuddled, Andrew looked up into Mr. Wormer's face and explained, "Sir, today's my birthday and I'm seven years old. Most of the boys go to work when they're ten." Andrew again kicked the dirt and said, "How am I to learn all that my mother spoke of in three years?"

Mr. Wormer paused a moment before saying, "Andrew, you and I will not finish in three years, for we want you to learn and appreciate Aristotle, Plato, and a new English playwright named William Shakespeare." Wormer looked deeply into Andrew's eyes and said, "To know and understand these people is to fly with the eagles and walk with God."

Disappointed, Andrew shifted his eyes away and stared at the ground.

Ranie pulled him close. "Andrew, you're a gentleman, and gentlemen run the world. I pray someday you will secure your rightful place, but for now you must prepare for that day."

"Yes, Mother. But all gentlemen have a last name. I don't have one."

"I know you don't, my son. What would you like to call yourself?" She hesitated, and then said, "You're an Englishman. How about Andrew English?"

"No, you're the only mother I've known. I'm your son. I'm Ranie's son." He smiled. When he repeated it, the words flowed from his mouth as "Andrew Ranson." They spilled out as if he always knew what it was to be.

"Oh, Andrew, what an honor!" Ranie's eyes welled up and a tear ran down her left cheek.

Mr. Wormer bowed and extended his right hand to Andrew. "Nice to make your acquaintance, Master Ranson."

With unpretentiousness, Andrew beamed and shook his hand. "Nice to make your acquaintance, sir."

Mr. Wormer told him, "Master Ranson, I'll be back tomorrow morning precisely at eight o'clock to commence your education. Perhaps I'll have a surprise for you."

Andrew, restless that night, thought, *Maybe he'll bring me a gift.*

The next morning at breakfast, Andrew didn't have much of an appetite. Pushing his porridge around in the bowl, he asked, "Mother, do you think Mr. Wormer will have a gift for me?"

"I don't know. But he will arrive soon." She kissed Andrew on the forehead. "You're going to love all the new things he will teach you."

Andrew, taking his last mouthful of porridge, thought, *Maybe this won't be too bad after all. Mother did say I'll be a gentleman someday. I have a last name, like a real gentleman. On the other hand, I already know how to read and write and lots of other stuff.*

The sound of horses' hooves interrupted his thoughts.

"He's here. Put a smile on your face, young man, and let us greet Mr. Wormer." Ranie sighed.

Ranie and Andrew watched Mr. Wormer help the driver slide a large trunk off the roof of the coach.

She shoved Andrew forward. "Son, go over and help him."

He tripped over his own feet. Regaining his balance, he approached Mr. Wormer and the driver as they were placing the trunk on the ground.

Pointing at the trunk, he asked, "Sir, are there presents in there for me?"

Mr. Wormer grinned. "Why, yes, Andrew, it contains gifts for your future. There's another trunk inside containing all my personal possessions. After I unpack, we will go for a long walk so we can get to know each other."

Andrew thought, *Maybe Mr. Wormer isn't so bad after all.* "Can we go down to the docks?" he asked. "I like to watch the ships coming and going. It's my most favorite place. I love hearing the sailors talking about strange lands and their wondrous adventures."

"It is exciting, Andrew. But for now, help me unpack."

✝✝✝

1662

Ranie announced to Mr. Wormer, "Andrew needs to learn to demonstrate his social graces at more than just children's parties, now that he's twelve years old."

"I couldn't agree with you more, Ms. Ranie. He is a good student. However, he is a loner and does need socializing. Did you have something in mind?"

"Yes. On May thirteenth I'll be taking him to the governor's celebration of Charles II reclaiming the throne as king of England, Scotland, and Ireland. I want you to teach him to dance and use proper manners."

"And who shall be his partner?"

"I know the perfect young lady for him to practice with. She's the child of the governor's wife's sister, and he has met her before."

One week later, Andrew and Mr. Wormer waited for the carriage to arrive with Miss Elizabeth, her chaperone, and Christopher, a musician with a violin. The minutes seemed like hours for Andrew; he nervously kept repeating the rules of behavior in his mind.

1) Both men and women must be dressed decently.

2) No man can dance in breeches and doublet without a coat.

3) Girls must not be thrown about.

When the carriage finally arrived, Andrew made the mandatory bow and repeated what he had endlessly rehearsed: "Miss Elizabeth, welcome to our home."

Andrew felt that she towered over him, even though she was only an inch or so taller. Golden-haired ringlets softly surrounded her rose-petal, doll-like face. She wore a long green dress that accentuated her mature breasts. The dress swished as they walked to the great room, where her chaperone sat on a nearby chair and the musician stood and waited by the fireplace.

Mr. Wormer instructed Andrew and Miss Elizabeth: "We will start with a Volta. It goes back to the thirteenth century. It has two steps, and high leaps assisted by the man. Touching each other in a dance is no longer frowned upon."

Andrew smiled and Elizabeth blushed.

Turning toward Christopher, Mr. Wormer said, "Please play the 'La Fallada.' "

The music began.

So it went, three days a week for three months. Andrew and Miss Elizabeth always exhibited proper English behavior. On the last day of practice, in order to lift her, he placed his hands below her waist, on her swaying hips. A sudden strange tingling sensation went through his body. Immediately he let go, dropping her to the floor.

Embarrassed and feeling like a scoundrel, he said, "Oh … oh … Miss Elizabeth, I'm s-sorry. I didn't mean to."

Elizabeth coyly smiled up at him. He bent down and helped her up. Watching his two young students, Mr. Wormer chuckled to himself.

She whispered, "Andrew, now you will have to marry me." She giggled.

"Oh, Elizabeth …."

"From now on, you may call me Bett."

This was the beginning of their close relationship.

Chapter 5

1666–1668
The Farm

Ranie's plan to increase the size of the farm by selling the future crops long before the harvest was successful. With the additional cash she bought more land, enabling her to plant and sell the combined crop.

Ranie's only day of rest and relaxation was Sunday. She, Mr. Wormer, and Andrew attended St. Paul's Church in Port Royal. After services, they'd go to their favorite inn and have lunch. After eating, they strolled to the marketplace on High Street. The street waslined with several small, attached, single-story, framed buildings that housed cobblers, wood turners, butchers, and bakers.

At the end of the street stood an old and large, two-story, red brick building. A swaying sign hung above the door, which read: "John Davis, Proprietor." One found the very best "salvaged" merchandise there. It was crammed full of bolts of silk and other fine fabrics that stuck out from the shelves. Silver and gold plates with matching goblets and trinkets covered the long wooden tables. The store contained the finest furniture, inlaid with rare woods and mother-of-pearl.

Andrew, bored with window-shopping, often slipped away from his companions and went to his favorite spot on Fishers' Row. There he would meet Bett.

They sat on the edge of the pier, watching the tall ships as the gentle sea breezes enveloped them, elevating their spirits.

One Sunday afternoon, Bett showed up limping.

Andrew stood to help her sit down. "What happened to you?" he asked.

"Oh, it's nothing."

Andrew blurted out, "Nothing? You can hardly walk!"

Sitting down, he put his arm around her.

She said, "Father purchased a beautiful new stallion. He warned me not to ride him because he was only half broken. I promised I wouldn't."

"But you——"

"The next day, I rode Samson."

"Why did you do that?"

"Oh, Andrew, he's magnificent—big and strong, like Samson. I knew he wanted me to ride him!"

"That's ridiculous. How did you know that?"

"No, you don't understand."

"You're right! I don't."

"Forget it. I'm a good rider. I saddled him up. When I got on him he reared, and I fell off. Luckily, I only twisted my ankle."

"What did your father say?"

"I don't want to talk about it."

"Oh, Bett, you shouldn't have gone against your father's wishes. Does your ankle hurt very much?"

"No."

He pulled her closer and gave her a kiss.

She blushed, and then he whispered into her ear, "I know a private place not far from here."

"Oh, Andrew, I don't kn——"

"It will be fine. No one will see us. There's an abandoned livery stable not far." He kissed her again and off they went.

Hay strewed the floor of the stable. In a corner was a pile about two feet high. Laughing, Andrew spread out his arms and ran and jumped onto it, shouting, "Bett, come here, don't be afraid." He threw some hay into the air.

Bett cautiously went over. Before she could say anything, Andrew grabbed her wrists and pulled her down as she giggled.

After hugging and kissing for a while, Andrew sat up and lifted his shirt over his head to brush off the hay that had gotten underneath.

Bett squealed, "Oh, Andrew ...." She covered her eyes. Her curiosity got the best of her and she peeked through her fingers.

Upon seeing his rosary, she asked, "Why do you wear a rosary around your neck?"

Fingering the cross, he said, "I have had this as long as I can remember. Ranie told me it belonged to my real mother."

"Oh. Who was she?"

"I don't know. Let's not talk about that now."

He gently caressed her face and pulled her toward him. As his hands roamed over her body, she experienced feelings that she had never felt before.

†††

Later that summer, Bett and Andrew sat enjoying the sea on a Sunday afternoon. The wind kicked up and blew Bett's hair into her face. Andrew gently pushed it back and kissed her cheek. The sea began to roar, the wind howled, and the blue-green ocean changed its calm personality into turmoil. The breaking waves became deafening.

Andrew's heart raced. He stood up, pointed, and shouted, "Look way out there, a waterspout!"

"Where?"

Pointing to a funnel cloud at sea, Andrew yelled, "Out there! A tornadic waterspout. They're dangerous!"

He extended his hand to help her up. They stood there staring at it for a moment.

"Bett, we have to go now."

"But I want to see …"

The sky darkened with cumulus clouds and the wind howled as it carried Bett's shaky voice: "You're right, we'd better go. I'll meet you next Sunday at our special place."

She gave Andrew a kiss and left to rejoin her parents.

Lightning streaked across the sky. Andrew headed for Fort Charles.

There he saw Ranie in their horse-drawn carriage, waving for him to come. A burst of thunder roared when he reached the carriage. The horses laid back their ears and their hooves pawed at the ground. Andrew jumped into the carriage and grabbed the reins from Ranie.

"Where's Mr. Wormer?"

Over the rumble of gale-force winds, Ranie shouted, "I couldn't find him. He wanders off some Sundays after church. I'm sure he'll be all right."

Another clap of thunder and a bolt of lightning, and they were off.

By the time they reached their barn, the wind-driven torrents had made their clothes a second skin.

"My son, I'll hold the horses while you open the barn door."

With a fierce wind blowing, Andrew struggled to pull one of the barn doors open. The wind ripped the door off its hinges and acted as a sail, lifting Andrew into the air, screaming. He came down head first next to a tree, knocking him unconscious.

"Oh my God!" Ranie shrieked, as she helplessly watched.

She drove the horses into the barn and ran to Andrew, hysterically shouting, "Are you all right, are you all right, my son?"

There was no response.

Tears ran down her cheeks. Her mind reeled. *This can't be happening!*

She grasped his wrists, caught her breath, and struggled to drag him into the nearby root cellar.

Leaning over Andrew, she said, "Can you hear me? Please answer me. It's your mother."

Her wet hair dripped on his face. He moaned when she moved to place his head in her lap.

She kissed his forehead and under her breath, said, "You're strong! You're not like the duchess." *Instantly, she hoped he hadn't heard her.*

As fast as the storm came, it was over.

When Andrew regained consciousness, Ranie said, "Thank God you're all right, my son."

"I'm fine, Mother. Are you all right?"

"Yes."

The two of them composed themselves.

Ranie asked, "If you're up to it, let us see what damage the storm did."

Courageously they walked out of the root cellar. To their shock, only two walls of the house remained. All the crops were lost. However, by a miracle, the barn and the horses survived.

Exasperated, Andrew kept repeating, "Oh my God! This can't be!" He turned to Ranie. "What do we do now?"

Ranie surveyed the situation and then looked to the heavens. Controlling her emotions, she took hold of Andrew's shoulders and calmly said, "My son, it is a test from God. We will start over again." Her mind all the time was racing, asking, *Why, why, dear God, did you do this to us!*

The following morning, the sun rose as if nothing had happened.

When they heard the sound of hooves approaching, Ranie and Andrew stopped sorting out their belongings.

A soldier mounted on a black stallion tipped his hat, looked down at them, and said, "Excuse me, Miss, I hate to bother you—"

Andrew broke in. "What do you want?"

The soldier cleared his throat and replied, "I've been told that you know Mr. Wormer."

Ranie wiped her hands on her apron, saying, "Bad storm, Mister, have a lot of work to do." Ranie wondered, *Why would a stranger want to know about Mr. Wormer?* She said, "Yes. Is he all right?"

You could hear the creaking of his saddle as the soldier moved uncomfortably and answered, "Sorry for your farm's loss, Miss." He paused.

Ranie responded curtly, "Thank you. What do you want?"

"Mr. Wor …"

Ranie's heart pounded.

He said, "Mr. Wormer didn't survive …"

Oh, dear God! "Andrew," she said, "it's … it's Mr. Wormer."

"I heard, Mother."

The stranger was saying, "… during the storm, he was in bed with a woman, when the roof fell in on top of them."

†††

Though exhausted, Ranie would not let anything stop her from reestablishing her farm. She knew she had to go to the moneylenders.

Struggling to keep her composure as she tied a shawl around her shoulders, she said, "Andrew, I'm going into town. I'll return in a few hours. Keep your eye on things."

Andrew put his arms around her. "I will. It will be all right."

She forced a smile and left.

The moneylenders were cordial but unmerciful; especially Mr. Rumford, whom Ranie had thought was on her side. Mr. Spindlier, whom she had never liked, was hard-nosed, tall, skinny, with peering beady black eyes.

Mr. Spindlier, without inflection, said, "Miss Ranie, we know you built your farm from nothing and made a success of it." He smirked, wrote something on a piece of paper, and continued. "We will help you."

He slipped the paper to Mr. Rumford, who gazed at it and nodded his approval. Mr. Rumford slid the paper across the table to Ranie.

Her eyes widened and she lifted a single eyebrow. The tone of her voice deepened when she bemoaned, "Good God! You must be jesting. This interest rate is much too high!"

"No, Miss Ranie—"

"B-but … it's … unreasonable."

"It is business, nothing personal, you understand," Rumford explained calmly.

She swallowed hard, trying to keep the venom from spewing out of her mouth. Through clenched teeth, she said, "I have no choice."

Chapter 6

1670
The *Cagway*

Andrew sat waiting impatiently for Bett at the pier. The churning ocean left droplets of moisture on his body.

She is taking too long, he thought. Becoming anxious, his mind went back to the time when Samson had reared and she fell off him.

The ocean roared.

He closed his eyes, placed his fingers over his mouth, and spoke aloud: "What if she—"

Over the rumblings of the ocean, he heard Bett's voice: "Andrew, my ..."

Startled, he looked up at her beautiful sweet face that now was torn with grief.

She sat down next to him. He put his arms around her. Her eyes filled with tears.

"What's the matter, my love?"

"It's my parents."

"What?"

She blurted out, "They won't let me see you anymore."

"Why?"

"They say you're penniless and will never amount to anything. They're going to marry me to a nobleman."

"No, Bett, I love you. They can't make you do that!"

"I told my parents it's you I love and I'd rather die than marry someone else. My father raged and threatened to send me to a convent if I didn't do as told." Bett sobbed, "What can I do?"

Andrew tried to comfort her. "Bett, it's God's plan for us to be together. Somehow, someday, it will work out. Never forget that."

She flung her arms around him and sighed. "I will always love you." She gave Andrew a soul-touching kiss.

He whispered, "Let's go to our special place."

†††

Jamaica suffered a terrible drought and Ranie's crops failed. She had sleepless nights; the moneylenders pressed her for payment, which she could not make.

Ranie snapped orders at Andrew to do things around the farm. Her demeanor had changed. He obeyed without questioning.

The impending foreclosure of her farm weighed heavily on her mind. Aggravated and frustrated, Ranie knew she must tell Andrew of their financial situation.

One evening while Ranie was washing the dishes and Andrew was drying them, she stopped, wiped her hands on her apron, and said, "Andrew I must tell you something."

"Mother, can't it wait?"

Her eyes swelled with tears.

"What's wrong?"

"My son, it's the moneylenders. They are taking everything except our clothes and family Bible."

Andrew gasped. "Can they ...? Why, those—"

"Andrew, what they're doing is legal."

"Where are we going to live?" he said in indignation.

Reassuring Andrew, Ranie went on. "We won't be homeless. I've been in contact with my cousin, Anne, in Kingston. She said she would shelter us."

"I'm not going. I'll stay here."

Troubled with his response, Ranie said, "Oh no, you're not!"

"I'm eighteen and educated. I can find a job. I know people in town. Once I have a job, I'll save enough money so we can buy another farm."

"But Andrew, you've never worked for anyone."

"So what?"

"You don't understand. It will not be like working with me."

"Mother, I have to be on my own sooner or later."

"You are a man." She shrugged her shoulders and said, "And not a little boy anymore. Do what you must."

Andrew kissed her. "Mother, if it doesn't work out, I promise I'll join you in Kingston."

A few days later, Ranie was packed and ready to leave for Kingston. Although she was worried, she gave an impression of confidence as she said good-bye.

†††

Looking for work was much harder than Andrew had thought. It seemed no one was interested in hiring such an educated person. The heat didn't make it any easier. His shirt clung to his body, sweat dripped down his face. Each step felt as if hundreds of pounds pressed down on him. Ranie's words kept turning in his head: *It is a test from God.* He was even more determined to get a job.

Andrew found himself in front of the Davis Salvage Shop. He knew that the narrow alley next to the shop led to the rear of the store, which had an overhang. There he could get out of the sun for a while. Exhausted, he propped up a box against the wall and sat down, closed his eyes, and, within seconds, fell into a deep sleep.

John Davis happened to be near the store's back door when he heard some noise. Cautiously peeking out, he was surprised to see Andrew. Davis had a strange sense of humor and thought it would be funny to throw a bucket of water on him.

Andrew, thinking he was drowning, flailed his arms about and awoke with a start, screaming, "Help! Help!"

Davis stood over him with the bucket in one hand and a cloth in the other. "Andrew, don't you get enough sleep? What are you doing here?" Davis threw him the cloth.

Andrew wiped his face, shook his head, and screeched, "What the hell ..."

"Woke yaw up, huh!" Davis laughed.

"Not funny. I've been looking for work for days and tried to get out of the sun for a few minutes."

"It's a job you need?"

"Yes. I need a job."

Davis ruminated a few moments, one hand rubbing his jaw. Thoughtfully, he said, "The rumors are true then, Miss Ranie and you lost the farm?"

Andrew stood up and, near tears, replied, "Yes, and I—"

Mr. Davis gripped Andrew's shoulders and yelled, "Those heartless moneylender bastards!"

Andrew's ears rang as Davis's voice boomed on: "You do realize you'll never make enough money, working for a living."

Andrew exhaled, casting his eyes down in despair, and stated, "It seems I'm overeducated ..."

Davis jumped in. "What can you do?"

Andrew looked up with a glimmer of hope and stated, "I speak four languages."

"My boy, you could work on a salvage ship. They make good wages. Every one of the crew gets a share of the profits."

"I never considered that!" Ranie's inner voice popped into his head: *My son, it's a test from God.* Andrew spontaneously hugged Mr. Davis.

Shocked by Andrew's reaction, he pulled back.

"Wonderful! That's perfect. I know how to plot a ship's course and read the stars."

"See, I thought that would be good for you."

Andrew lowered his voice, saying, "However, I don't know anything about sailing."

Davis stepped forward and put his arm around the damp Andrew. "Don't worry," he said, "you're intelligent and well educated. The officers will teach you everything you need to know on the ship."

"When can I start?"

"The captain is not on board now, but I know Billy Pierson, the quartermaster on the salvage brig, the *Cagway*, and it's in dock. I'll send word to him to expect you tomorrow."

Andrew forgot about the heat and wanted to throw his arms around Davis again, but this time restrained himself and effusively said, "That's wonderful of you, Mr. Davis."

"My pleasure, Andrew. I wish you the best." Davis slipped a hand into his pants pocket, pulled out a pound note, and gave it to Andrew.

"You don't have to do this …"

"Have a good dinner and stop worrying."

After shaking hands, Andrew left and went to his favorite pub.

†††

Down on the wharf the next day, Andrew stood only a few feet away from the impressive *Cagway*. He estimated the ship to be two hundred feet long, with masts over one hundred feet high. Captivated, Andrew watched the crew of sailors cleaning ten short black iron cannons that stuck out from below the main deck. He watched in fascination as he scrutinized the men. The energy of the bustling sailors unloading cargo off the ship excited him.

He called out to them, "Where's Mr. Pierson?"

A sailor stopped what he was doing, wiped his brow with a sweaty forearm, and yelled back, "He's on the sterncastle."

"Where's that?"

Looking at Andrew, the sailor thought the young man a landlubber of the first order. He shook his head, pinched his tufted eyebrows together, turned, and pointed up to a weather-beaten, short, stout, middle-aged man standing on the raised part at the rear of the ship. The sailor cupped his hands around his mouth and shouted, "Mr. Pierson, there's someone here to see you!"

Mr. Pierson looked around and after a moment saw where the voice came from. Looking down at the dock he called out, "Is it Andrew Ranson?"

Andrew hollered, "Yes, it's me, sir."

"Come aboard," Pierson barked out.

Andrew sucked in the air, swallowed hard, threw his shoulders back, and proceeded up the gangway as it rattled and creaked.

Upon Andrew's reaching the deck, another sailor said loudly, "Ahoy, there. Mr. Pierson told me to show you to his quarters. Follow me."

Andrew smiled and followed. His mind reeled with questions.

Stopping at the door, Andrew's heart pounded. The sailor opened it and Andrew went in. The sailor turned and slammed the door shut before Andrew could say good-bye. The ship swayed to the rhythm of the sea. A hammock hung swinging in the corner of the small, dingy room. A suspended oil lamp squeaked over a table covered with charts and papers. The sound of the cabin door opening startled Andrew as he tried to stay erect on the swaying ship.

Mr. Pierson stood there, cleared his throat, and then bellowed, "Well, Mr. Andrew Ranson, we are extremely busy."

Andrew could see the annoyance in his face.

Scratching his head and rolling his nerve-jarring eyes, Mr. Pierson said, "The captain told me you're an extremely important addition to our crew!"

Andrew puffed his chest out.

Mr. Pierson ranted, "What's your background? How can we use you? Who the hell are you, anyway?"

No one had ever spoken to him in such a manner.

Andrew composed himself and said, "I can use an astrolabe. I know higher mathematics, and can read and write in four languages."

"Do yaw know Spanish?"

"Spanish, French, and Dutch."

"Perfect, you can assist our sailing master. He's responsible for the navigation of the ship and correction of inaccurate charts. In some areas, charts are nonexistent. In two days, we sail." Mr. Pierson went over to the table, picked up some papers, handed them to Andrew, and said, "First you must agree to these ship's articles by making your mark."

"Yes, sir." Andrew thumbed through and read one page aloud, which contained articles on how the sailors were to behave on the ship. Starting from the most important,

There is to be:
NO Stealing from Each Other
No Women Allowed
No Excessive Drunkenness
Strict Compliance to the orders of the Captain and his Officers.

The last few pages had the men's signatures. He estimated about one hundred sailors aboard had signed their names with an X.

With great pride in his handwriting, he penned his name in cursive letters: *Andrew Ranson*, then shook hands with Mr. Pierson, and left the ship.

Once in town, Andrew sent word by the Royal Mail to Ranie that everything was all right. He gathered his belongings to join the ship. He would try to forget Bett and concentrate on his future.

Chapter 7

1670–1671
Lady Elizabeth Loxley

Bett's idealistic life in Jamaica ended when her parents, claiming to have her best interests in mind, arranged a marriage through Lady Margot West, who knew Lord Edward Loxley. A close friend to Bett's parents, Lady Margot West introduced Bett's parents to His Lordship and negotiated the marriage contract.

When Bett's parents presented the arrangement to her, she became hysterical, saying, "I'm not going to marry him! I love Andrew."

Her father raised his hand as if to hit her, but constrained himself while spurting out, "I don't want to hear such nonsense. He is a titled English gentleman. You will marry him."

Sticking her chin out and stiffening her back, she placed her hands on her hips in protest. "I will not! I love Andrew."

Her father scowled and retorted, "That's enough out of you, young lady. You don't know what's best for you. That's why these matters are left to older and wiser heads."

Bett pleaded, "Mother, you know I love Andrew."

Her mother stood there just staring at the floor.

Her father wagged his finger at Bett, resolute in his decision. "You will marry Lord Edward Loxley and that's final!"

Grabbing his wife by the hand, they walked out of the room.

Bett lost interest in her appearance, gained weight, and rarely left her home. In spite of her rebellion, her parents had the marriage performed by proxy.

†††

Weeks later, Lord Loxley arrived in high spirits. Upon meeting Bett for the first time, he reached for her hand; she cast her eyes toward the floor, and took a small step back.

"Good to finally meet you, my dear. May I address you as Beth or Bett?"

Her head pounded, her mind screamed: *No, no, this can't happen! I love Andrew!* Her eyes welled with tears.

Pulling her hand away, she curtly answered, "No, only one person calls me Bett."

"Then what shall I call you, dear?"

With narrowed eyes and puckered lips she answered, "Elizabeth will do."

Smirking, he said, "Elizabeth, it shall be." With lust in his eyes, he grabbed her right hand, put it up to his lips, and lightly kissed it. "My dear, there's nothing to fear."

Her stomach turned as he continued: "Now that we're husband and wife, we're the guests of the First Lord of the Admiralty on a Royal Navy frigate, which will take us to England."

Bett sighed.

†††

The captain and his officers invited the Loxleys to the customary first night's dinner. He made a formal toast for this special occasion.

With raised glass, he said, "An English blessing for the bride and groom: May your joys be as sweet as spring flowers that grow / As bright as a fire when winter winds blow / As countless as leaves that float down in the fall / As serene as the love that keeps watch over us all."

Everyone raised their glass and cheered, "Hear, hear!"

Lady Elizabeth picked at her food; Lord Loxley inhaled his. After dinner, not feeling well, she excused herself. Looking at his new wife, Loxley glowered and clenched his lips. The look on his face unnerved her. She faked a smile, turned, and left for their cabin.

Loxley swallowed his wine and stated, "I'll be with you soon. Do prepare yourself."

Her skin crawled upon her hearing those words and she became nauseous walking to the cabin. Exhausted, she washed and changed into her white nightgown while dreading the coming encounter. Nervously she collapsed onto the bed and eventually fell into a deep sleep.

Loxley stayed in the captain's quarters to play a card game called sheepshead.

Hours later, an unfamiliar noise awoke her.

"Who's there?" Lady Elizabeth called out.

"Quiet, wife!" Loxley yelled. He rummaged through the dresser drawers, throwing things around, shouting, "Where's the key? I have to settle my debts with the captain and the boys."

The room filled with tension. Elizabeth could see beads of perspiration dripping down into his drink-squinted black eyes. Wiping the sweat with his shirtsleeve, he stopped abruptly, cast an irate glance at Elizabeth, and repeated, "Girl, where's the damn key?"

Terrified, she sat up, pulling the covers up close to her chest. "What are you doing? What are you talking about?"

He stumbled toward her.

Her gut knotted, she retreated deeper into the covers, with only her panic-struck eyes peeping out. Speaking through the covers her voice choked, "You're drunk!"

Lord Edward Loxley took another step closer, his fur-thick eyebrows arched over his bloodshot eyes. He loomed over her.

She screamed, "Stay away from me!"

"Don't you talk to me like that!" He slapped her across the face. "Now, where's that damn key?"

Through her tears she said, "I'm not telling you."

His massive hand came toward her again.

"No, don't …."

She let go of the cover and reached to the back of her neck to unclasp the long, thin, silver chain from which a small key dangled. Before she could undo the clasp, Loxley grabbed the chain and yanked it.

Sobbing and barely audible, she whimpered, "Take it. It's all yours anyway. Leave me alone!"

Loxley's cumbersome fingers tightened around the key. The chain fell to the floor. He lumbered over to the chest that held her dowry. Loxley's fingers fumbled, trying to place the small key into the chest's lock. Frustrated, he cursed foully, betraying his breeding despite his position in life. Finally, after a few more moments, he opened the chest and grabbed a large handful of English pound notes.

He turned and gave his bride a menacing look and growled, "When I get back, you better be naked."

He walked out, slamming the cabin door. Lady Elizabeth sobbed. Thoughts of her gentle Andrew passed through her mind.

It wasn't long before fear flooded over her when she heard footsteps approaching the door. Loxley burst through the doorway. Her heart pounded. He glared at his new bride and the lines between his eyes deepened into dark crevices.

His words fanned his smoldering anger: "I told you to be naked when I got back!"

Staggering over to the bed, he slapped her face. Her left cheek immediately swelled. She screamed. Loxley ripped off her nightdress; he grabbed her arms and pulled her up to a standing position while tears streamed down her face. Putting his huge, sweaty hands on her shoulders, he turned her around and pushed her torso across the bed, while her feet were still on the floor.

She cried and pleaded, "No! Please don't!"

He kicked her legs apart, and then violently and repeatedly took her from behind.

Her torturous screams were heard throughout the ship. Her shrieks ignited the sailors' imaginations.

The lieutenant turned to the captain, laughing. "He must be shagging her good."

When Loxley finished, he collapsed on top of her in a drunken stupor. She struggled to get free from under his massive body. Crying softly, covering her intimate parts with her hands, she huddled in a wingback chair.

At midday, Loxley awoke to Lady Elizabeth standing over him with two knitting needles clenched in one hand.

Loxley was only half-awake when she stated, "My husband, I'll be Lady Loxley. I'll run your home. I'll attend functions for and with you. You can have all the whores you want, but if you ever touch me again I swear I will put one of these knitting needles through your eyes when you're asleep, and poison your food."

He nodded and uttered a few undistinguishable words and fell back to sleep.

†††

Three months later, Lord Loxley came home late at night, stumbling and yelling profanities. Lady Elizabeth awoke and went to top of the landing where the smell of cheap perfume wafted up from him. She held on to the banister, looked down, and saw him swaying at the foot of the stairwell. Her energy welled up within her.

She heard herself say, with bursting force, "You misbegotten son of Satan, your seed grows within me."

"What are you talking about, woman?"

"I'm with child."

Lord Loxley's eyes widened. He shook his head in disbelief.

"It's true," she yelled, with tears running down her cheeks.

"I'm going to be a father. An heir to my title … how nice."

He proceeded to pull his bloated body up the steps. Reaching the top, he made an effort to kiss Lady Elizabeth, but she avoided him by stepping backward. Annoyed at her response, he shoved her aside with one hand and continued to his bedroom.

Flopping onto his bed he repeated, "I'm going to be a father."

Chapter 8

1668–1672
A New Life

Andrew had mixed emotions while walking up *Cagway*'s creaking gangway. Stepping onto the deck, he could feel the sting of salt air on his face. The breezes blew his hair. He stopped for a moment and watched the ocean swells. Sea gulls flew and squawked around the ship; pelicans effortlessly dove into the water and came up with fish.

His mind spun. *Am I doing the right thing, or should I have stayed with Ranie?*

His heart longed for Bett. He reflected on the times when they had watched the great ships and dreamed of a life together.

A couple of boisterous sailors came up the gangway and jolted Andrew back to reality. He proceeded directly to his quarters, one deck below.

Pausing at the door, he smiled to himself and thought, *I'm about to begin my new life.*

When Andrew unlatched the door, a sudden swell caused the ship to roll and he lost his footing. *I'm going to have to get used to new experiences,* he mused.

He gazed around the room, went over to his hammock, and threw his haversack on it. At that moment there was a knock on the door. Before Andrew could say "Come in," the door opened.

"Captain Robert Searle wants to see you."

A beehive of activity surrounded them as they made their way to the captain's cabin. Andrew restrained himself from asking questions.

The captain's quarters were below the sterncastle. There the captain stood looking out of the large window at the rear of the ship.

The captain slowly turned around and said, "Andrew."

"Yes, sir."

"Please sit down."

The bright sunlight streaming through the window outlined the lanky figure to an indistinguishable profile; however, the voice sounded familiar.

"Andrew, I know you're highly educated and can speak a variety of languages." He walked closer and said, "This ship needs an intelligent young man like you to supplement my officers."

Stunned, Andrew cocked his head in disbelief, realizing the notorious Captain Robert Searle was John Davis, the seller of salvaged goods in Port Royal.

Andrew replied, "M-Mr. D-Davis …."

"Andrew, on this ship it's Captain Searle or Captain."

"Yes, Captain, I understand." A sudden coldness hit Andrew to his core.

A boom of laughter came from the captain. "Now, Andrew, you will be the navigator's assistant. I need you to sail captured ships to Port Royal. When you're on the *Cagway*, I also will use you to negotiate with anyone we may encounter who doesn't speak English. If there is resistance, you will go below deck with Mr. Doyle, my navigator, where you'll both be safe. If we fall to the Spanish or get lost at sea, the worst is to lose the ship's navigator. Do you understand? The two of you are never to be at risk."

Ducking his chin, Andrew responded, "Is this a pirate ship?"

"No, a privateer. I carry a Letter of Marque, a commission that legally permits us to wreak havoc on Spanish possessions for profit. Now go and find my navigator, Mr. Doyle. He knows you're on board. We sail with the outgoing tide."

††

Sailing south by southwest for three days, the *Cagway* came across a Spanish merchant ship.

Standing on the sterncastle, Mr. Doyle and Andrew intently watched Captain Searle maneuver the ship.

Remembering the captain's words, *'The two of you are never to be at risk,'* Andrew asked, "Shouldn't we go below?"

"No, not yet. Watch and learn."

Captain Searle's senses heightened once the *Cagway* maneuvered alongside the merchant ship. He ordered the colors struck and the black flag hoisted. Upon seeing it, the merchant ship turned downwind to get away. The pressure of the wind on its sails caused their ship to heel over, exposing part of the hull that's normally underwater. Immediately, the *Cagway* drew windward and fired a single warning shot across her bow. Knowing there was no escape, the merchant's captain dropped their sails, raised a white flag, and surrendered without a fight.

After boarding the merchant ship, Captain Searle shouted to lower a few small boats so the merchant crew could leave in peace. Once they were in the boats, he threw down a compass, some food, and a jug of water.

Watching the boats sail away, Andrew felt uneasy. "How did you know this was going to happen?" he asked the navigator.

Doyle leaned on the railing and professed, "All captains know that if they surrender to us without a fight, no one will be harmed. Our captain is only interested in selling the ship and its contents for profit."

After taking a complete inventory of the contents, Captain Searle went back to the *Cagway*. He gave Andrew twenty-five of his best men to sail the captured merchant ship to Port Royal, while he scouted out the defenses of Vera Cruz.

After docking the ship in Port Royal, Andrew sent word to Ranie that he would visit in a few days.

†††

Andrew arrived in a coach at Port Royal. He could see Ranie holding her skirt down from the wind as the sun reflected the bright colors of her tightly tied head scarf. The sight of her made him yearn to go back to happier times.

The moment Andrew's foot touched the ground, Ranie ran over to him, throwing her arms about him.

Before she could say a word, he spoke. "Mother, I've missed you so!"

A tear ran down her cheek, even though she held back a plethora of emotions.

Releasing him, she wiped her tears and held him at arm's length, "Look at you, my son, a sailor."

He smiled, and she went on: "My darling boy, in celebration of your return, Cousin Anne and I prepared your favorite dinner."

"Partridge! Oh, how I've had a hunger for it."

Cousin Anne was overjoyed to see Andrew, as he was to see her. They embraced.

"Andrew I'm glad you've come home. Your mother and I—"

"I know, I can smell the partridge."

She glanced at Ranie, and they both smiled.

Anne pointed to some chairs next to the fireplace. "Why don't you both sit down and catch up while I finish making dinner."

Andrew put his haversack alongside his chair. He bragged on how he had become an assistant navigator. He did not mention that the ship was a privateer with a Letter of Marque to prey on the Spanish. However, he did mention he never lost faith in God. Ranie listened intently, swelling with pride.

Before Ranie could say anything, Andrew declared, "My heart aches for Bett, Mother. I must see her."

Ranie stood up, went over to him, and put her arm around his shoulders. "Andrew, there are many things beyond one's control ...."

Andrew looked into her eyes and said, "What are you talking about?"

Trying to find the right words, Ranie sighed and said, "Bett ... Bett is married."

He jumped up. "What!"

"She's married."

"That can't be true."

Ranie spoke with a broken heart. "Her father arranged her marriage to Lord Loxley."

"No!" Andrew exclaimed, running his fingers through his hair.

"They live in England."

At that moment Cousin Anne announced, "Dinner is ready."

Andrew's shoulders slumped; the reality of Bett's marriage started to sink in. He picked up his haversack, shook his head in disbelief, and proceeded to the table. He placed his bag next to the chair.

Observing Andrew only pick at his favorite meal, Anne said, "Dear boy, you're not eating. Are you not feeling well? Your mother and I made it especially for you. What's wrong?"

Ranie answered for him. "Oh, Anne, he's tired."

Andrew politely smiled.

After dinner, Andrew mechanically reached into his haversack, pulled out a set of rolled-up parchment papers, and spread them out on the table.

"What's this, my dear son?"

Pointing to them, he explained: "Mother, your future."

"What are you talking about?"

He placed his hands on the documents and went on. "These documents state that I am giving you a portion of my share of my voyage profits."

"Oh, Andrew ...."

"Mother, I need quill and ink. I must change something in the document."

Before Ranie could move, Cousin Anne got up and fetched the needed implements.

Andrew searched for the words to write in the document: *My mother Ranie is to receive half of my profits.* Dipping the quill into the ink, he drew a line through the word *half,* then inserted the word *all,* and initialed the change. "This should give you enough money to purchase a new farm."

Ranie was shaking with excitement. "Good heavens, Andrew, it will be wonderful for us to be together again."

"No, Mother, I'm going back to sea."

Chapter 9

1675
Abigail's Birthday

Lord Loxley's schedule never varied:

Mondays – He awoke at noon, went to his club, drank, and gambled into the night.

Tuesdays – Out of bed at noon, visited one of his favorite whores, and went to a pub, drank and gambled until late at night.

Wednesdays – Slept again until noon, went to the public racecourse, gambled, drank, and of course visited another one of his whores.

On Thursdays and Fridays – He repeated the schedules of Mondays and Tuesdays.

Saturdays – Devoted to hunting.

Sundays – He got up early, shaved and dressed impeccably in order to accompany Bett and their daughter, Abigail, to church. There, he was a shining example, a pillar of society, and gave generously to all causes.

After services, parishioners went out of their way to shake his hand and praise the Loxley family.

Lady Elizabeth was careful that her responses did not betray her. She thought, *What an actor he is. I'm the only one who knows the truth.* She'd smile sweetly and sigh, "Yes, I'm so lucky."

When he'd start jiggling his leg, she knew it was a sign of his impatience and that he wanted to leave to play cards with his so-called friends.

†††

Lady Elizabeth made elaborate plans for a grand party to celebrate her daughter's fourth birthday.

The manor was full of happy activity the day before the event.

Abigail's eyes sparkled, and she giggled, saying, "Mommy, will Daddy be at my party tomorrow?"

Lord Loxley had promised Lady Elizabeth he would attend and be on his best behavior.

"Yes, dear, now go and play."

She dropped a light kiss on her forehead. Abigail smiled and left.

That evening at Abigail's bedtime, Lady Elizabeth tucked her precious child in and told her, "Now go to sleep, because when you wake you will be four years old."

"I'll be a big girl."

"Yes, dear. Now go to sleep."

Lady Elizabeth waited in vain for her husband to come home that night.

The next afternoon, Abigail excitedly bounced up and down as her mother tried to dress her for the birthday party.

"Stand still, dear. The—"

Abigail gleefully yelled, "Mommy, I can hear my favorite song, 'London Bridge Is Falling Down.'"

"Yes, the musicians are getting ready to play for your party."

Spinning in a circle to the music, Abigail breathlessly shouted, "I can't wait to get all my presents."

Lady Elizabeth clasped her hands and said, "Abigail, you must—"

Abigail abruptly stopped and exclaimed, "Mommy, where's Daddy?"

Elizabeth's stomach tensed. She suppressed an impatient huff and said, "I'm sure he'll be here, dear. Now let's finish getting you dressed."

Holding hands, Elizabeth and her daughter proceeded to the upper landing of the grand staircase, where Elizabeth paused for a moment, looking over the crowd for her husband.

Abigail squealed, "Mommy, you're hurting me."

Proceeding down the staircase, Abigail tugged at her mother's dress and whispered, "Where's Daddy? Isn't he coming?"

Elizabeth sighed and said, "He'll be here, my pet. Let's go greet our guests."

Abigail stood next to her mother when she explained to the guests, "I'm sorry, my dear friends, that an emergency has occurred and His Lordship will not be able to join us."

Some of the guests gasped.

Lady Elizabeth went on: "One of our tenant farmers' daughters suddenly got sick. So, my friends, my compassionate husband undertook the responsibility of taking her to our personal physician."

Abigail whined, "Who's sick, Mommy?"

"Shush, pet."

Someone called out, "How kind, considerate, and charitable of him."

Lady Elizabeth batted her eyes, cocked her head, and responded, "Yes, I'm very lucky. Now, everyone, enjoy yourselves."

Later on, there was a commotion at the door. Clothes in disarray, eyes bloodshot, and reeking of liquor, Lord Loxley stumbled in, carrying a large wrapped gift.

Flaring his arms, he staggered deeper into the crowd, bellowing and slurring his words: "I'm sooorrry. Now, where's the birthday girl?"

A hush fell over the room.

He put the gift down, knelt to the floor, and shrieked, "Where's my birthday girl?" He sang at the top of his lungs, "Happy birthday, my loving daughter, dear Abigail, where are you?" Abruptly he stopped, stood up, spread his arms, and screeched, "Abigail, come and give your father a big hug and kiss."

The guests tittered nervously while little Abigail hid behind her mother's skirt and sobbed hysterically.

Lady Elizabeth picked her up, wiped her tears, kissed her, and said, "Your father is not feeling well, dear."

Abigail continued to cry.

Lady Elizabeth stood with her feet planted firm; her pulse increased. Her voice deepened: "It's better you leave now, my dear husband!"

The guests scattered. Loxley picked up his package and lumbered over to a high-backed wing chair.

Flopping into it, he scowled and rambled on: "It's MY daughter's birthday party." Flailing his hands wildly, he bellowed, "Let's all have a drink and celebrate," and then he passed out.

Hours later, Loxley woke up screaming, "Where the hell's everyone?"

††††

A few days later, one of the servants interrupted Lady Elizabeth as she sat engrossed in her needlework, notifying her that Mr. Nickels, Loxley's tailor, had arrived without an appointment and wanted to see His Lordship immediately.

Lady Elizabeth put her work down, straightened out her dress as she stood, and said, "Tell Mr. Nickels that Lord Loxley is not in residence at present." She paused and added, "However, I will see him. Send him to the library. I'll be there shortly."

Her muscles tensed. Puzzled as to why he had come uninvited, she went to meet him.

Mr. Nickels was tall and impeccably dressed. He bowed his head in respect as Elizabeth entered.

"Please sit down, Mr. Nickels."

"That won't be necessary, it will take but a moment. Your Ladyship, this concerns financial matters, and therefore I must speak to His Lordship."

"That's impossible. He will be away for a few weeks on business."

"I'm embarrassed to bring this up, Lady Elizabeth, however, Lord Loxley's accountant failed to remit payment for the last quarter. I do need payment."

She blushed and her words spilled out: "Mr. Nickels, I do apologize for the oversight. Be assured you will be paid."

Within the following weeks, other incidents of missed payments came to her attention. Worried and not wanting herself and Abigail to end up in the poorhouse, she went to Mr. Wilson, the estate's accountant, to find out the details of their finances.

Lady Elizabeth held her chin high, and heat flushed through her body even though it was a cool day when she entered Mr. Wilson's office. She flashed a false smile when his small bald head popped up to regard her from behind the huge desk.

He said, "Please take a seat, Lady Elizabeth."

Her eyes narrowed as she watched him remove his pince-nez glasses.

Before he could put his spectacles down on top of a pile of papers, she stated, "Mr. Wilson, I must know the state of my finances."

"Oh!" Rubbing his head while trying to search for the right words, he said, "Please, s-sit down, Lady Loxley. ... I have been meaning to talk to you."

Her hands became clammy as he went on.

"I fear I must tell Your Ladyship that Lord Loxley has fallen on somewhat hard times."

Her throat tightened, her limbs tingled. She wanted to flee.

"His Lordship has been spending the estate's income at an alarming rate. Only last week, invoices arrived in excess of triple the normal amount. We had no plans for items such as the jewelry he purchased for you."

She thought, *What jewelry? That son of Satan, he didn't buy me jewelry.*

Mr. Wilson said, "In fact, if possible, I might go so far as to suggest Your Ladyship may wish to return any such items for which you have not developed a fondness. If you do so, it's my hope such proceeds, in addition to the back rents from the estate tenants, would enable you to continue as you are—provided Your Ladyship can bring Lord Loxley to a more careful management of his expenditures. I fear he has paid no heed to my repeated request for moderation. If he continues on the current path, it may become necessary to sell your townhome or some other possessions."

Elizabeth leaned forward, putting her hands firmly on the desk and, aghast at what their accountant had revealed, promised she would discuss the situation with her husband and commence with the proper action.

†††

Lady Elizabeth spent sleepless nights thinking about the horrendous state of their finances.

One restless night, she awoke with the answer whispering in her mind, and said to herself, "That's it. I'll take care of it first thing in the morning." Satisfied, she rolled over and had the first good sleep in many nights.

In the morning, she went to the estate's solicitor and explained that her husband was very ill and therefore unable to seek him out. Lord Loxley, however, had confessed to her that he had fallen under the influence of an unscrupulous person, which had deleterious repercussions on the estate's income.

She asked if she could draw up documents that would give temporary control of all estate matters into her hands. Lady Elizabeth indicated she and her husband had conceived of such an action to thwart the unscrupulous man.

Shocked by the request, the solicitor agreed it was possible to devise such documents—though highly unusual. He urged her to consider seriously the burden of such responsibilities, as they were not appropriate for a woman.

Lady Elizabeth assured him that her husband was eager for relief and would advise her in all aspects. After all, it was only temporary; she would sign new documents returning control to her husband when the danger had passed.

After hearing this, the solicitor said, "I shall draw up the papers immediately."

Upon receiving the documents, Lady Elizabeth knew she had to wait for the right moment to ask Loxley to sign.

†††

A few days later, Loxley came home extremely intoxicated. He opened her bedroom door and shuffled over to the bed.

Drooling over her, he sneered and said, "I'm here, my reticent love. You won't put me off this time. I've come to claim my husbandly rights, whether you like it or not. After all, I expect a male heir."

Her stomach turned; however, she instinctively knew this was her chance.

Lady Elizabeth smiled sweetly and patted the bed, cooing, "Dear, lie down next to me."

As he promptly did so, she leapt out of bed and said, "Dear, stay there, close your eyes. I have a surprise for you."

She went over to the desk where a decanter of wine sat, poured some into a glass, and took it to Loxley.

"Thank you, my dear."

She smiled, and as he sipped, she returned to the desk, where a quill and inkpot sat. She removed the document from the drawer and dipped the quill into the inkpot.

While he was still sipping his wine, she blurted out, "Our bills are not being paid. Tradesmen are charging us much too much. You've not been paying attention to the estate's business. You're always gambling! It won't be long before we'll both be in the poorhouse. I talked about the situation with our solicitor. He drew up these documents, putting financial matters in my name, temporarily, of course."

Her husband laughed.

She went on. "This is what you're going to do." Holding out the legal paper in front of him, Lady Elizabeth declared, "This document gives me the exclusive authority to run our estate and make all the business decisions."

Loxley limbered up his shoulders and neck as if preparing for a fight. His eyebrows arched almost to his forehead. His eyes widened with disbelief and he boomed, "What the hel—"

"I'll arrange for you to have enough money to continue your lifestyle." She shoved the paper and quill into his hand. "Now, sign this!"

Throwing the glass against the fireplace, he snapped, "A woman doing business!"

"Sign here!" she said, pointing to a blank signature line.

Jabbing his finger in her face as adrenaline rushed through his body, a guttural roar came from him: "Never!"

"Never, you say," she said, mimicking him. "If you don't sign, you will wake up one morning in a pool of your own blood because your manhood will be gone!"

"You wouldn't dare!"

Looking directly at him, defiantly she retorted, "Do you really want to find out?"

"All right, I will sign it under duress. But you'll pay for this."

✝✝✝

Months passed, and the dammed-up, simmering hatred for his wife boiled over. One summer night there was a thunderstorm. Winds howled and bolts of lightning zigzagged across the midnight sky when a drunken Loxley banged on the door with one hand while holding onto his hat with the other.

One of the servants opened the door to Loxley, who was dripping wet.

"Get out of my way," he commanded, pushing the servant aside.

The servant lost his balance and fell.

Looking down at him, Loxley growled, "What the hell are you doing down there? Get up."

The servant rose and composed himself. He asked, "Sir, may I remove your things?"

Ignoring him, Loxley made his way to the study. Going over to his massive hand-carved desk, he muttered to himself, "Who the hell does she think she is! I am the man and I do as I please."

Pausing in front of his desk for a moment, barely able to insert the key, he managed to open the drawer and rifled through it.

Loxley pulled out a pistol. "I'll fix her!"

He stuck the pistol into the waist of his pants, and proceeded to the stairwell, yelling, "I want my wife. Where's my beautiful wife?"

Elizabeth heard the commotion downstairs, but ignored it because she was in her daughter's room trying to soothe Abigail's nightmare.

"Pet, it's all right, it's only a bad dream. Close your eyes and go back to sleep."

Hugging her mother, Abigail asked, "Is that Daddy?"

"Hush, pet. I'll go and see. Now go to sleep," she said, and then kissed Abigail on a rosy cheek.

When Elizabeth got to the landing, Lord Loxley was halfway up. Standing there, she looked down at him and put a finger to her lips. "Shush, Abigail's awake."

When Loxley pulled himself up another step, she could see the rage in his eyes.

Only one step away and hanging onto the banister with his left hand, he drew the pistol from his waistband and commanded, "Get down on your knees, you bitch!"

"No! You're drunk!"

"Get closer to the edge of the step and get down on your knees, or I will shoot you right now."

Elizabeth's heart accelerated and her stomach knotted. Afraid of his tyrannical temper, she took a small step forward and knelt down. Loxley held on to the railing with his left hand, swaying.

Placing the pistol to her head with his right hand, he ordered, "Now open your mouth!"

He let go of the railing to unbutton his trousers. With that, he fell backward.

†††

The investigation had only one witness. All the servants in the manor said they did not see or hear anything. Lady Elizabeth Loxley's testimony was short and simple.

"I was with my daughter in her room on the second floor. Lord Loxley must have thought he heard an intruder. He grabbed his pistol and went downstairs to look around. The next thing I heard was my loving husband, Lord Loxley, yelling out, 'Help!' "

Sobbing, she continued: "I left Abigail's room and went to the staircase, where Lord Loxley was coming up. Almost at the top step, he said, 'I'm dizzy.' He suddenly swayed and fell backward."

The sheriff, knowing the nature of Lord Loxley, looked at Lady Elizabeth, grinned inwardly, and mellifluously said, "My condolences, Lady Loxley. It's obvious this was a terrible accident."

He thanked her for her cooperation, and closed the investigation.

Chapter 10

Life at Sea

The navigator, Mr. Doyle, instructed Andrew in the accepted behavior of men at sea. Robert Whitefish, a recent addition to the crew, befriended Andrew. Like Andrew, it was his first time aboard a salvage ship; however, that was all they had in common.

The first three days had been smooth, easy sailing for Mr. Whitefish. On the fourth, the sea's temperament changed. Swells grew and forceful waves hit the ship. Three decks below, Robert Whitefish was working alone. The rocking and rolling upset him; he felt his lunch coming up to his throat, and his belly rumbled as it cramped. His skin turned pasty. Needing to relieve himself immediately, he thought of Mr. Doyle's orders: *"Get to the top deck, where you would squat over the railing, or go to the stern of the ship, where there's a hole cut in the deck, which allows one's waste to drop into the ocean."* Knowing he would not make it, he spotted an empty bucket and thought, *I'll do it in there and later I'll dump it overboard.* After relieving himself, he felt much better and color returned to his face. He carefully slid the bucket into the corner.

An hour or so later, a ship's officer came down to inspect the hold of the ship. The ship always had a stink about it; however, today it was worse. He followed the sickening odor and, upon seeing the bucket, his stomach turned.

He shouted, "Who's responsible for this shit?"

Dropping what he was doing, Robert Whitefish went over to the officer and said, "Sir, I am sorry. I could not wait. I was going to thro—"

"Belay that talk! This is a very serious matter, Mister. You've read the ship's articles of personal cleanliness?"

"Ye—"

The officer gave him a sharp eye. "This could cause disease to spread throughout the ship."

"I'm sor—"

"I'm putting you on report," the officer told him.

Word spread around the ship that Robert Whitefish was in trouble and would suffer the consequences.

Upon hearing the news, Andrew felt bad for Whitefish. Expressing his feelings to Mr. Doyle, he said, "Sir, I don't think you should be hard on Whitefish."

"And what business is it of yours?"

"Eh, sir, Whitefish was sick. He did his job and was going to dump it overboard when he finished his chores."

Mr. Doyle snapped, "That's not the point, Mr. Ranson. The two most dangerous things on a ship are fire and disease. In Whitefish's case, the shit—"

"You mean excrement ..."

Mr. Doyle screamed, "Don't you ever correct me! The shit could have spread sickness. The entire crew could have died!"

Andrew asked, "What will the captain do?"

Mr. Doyle rubbed his chin, then turned away and looked up at the sky for a moment. Turning back to Andrew, he said, "Ain't it a damn shame we're not birds? We could do it from the air and no one could stop us."

Andrew chuckled, breaking the tension.

Doyle's demeanor changed. "It's not a laughing matter. This is serious, and Whitefish could be marooned or keelhauled. Most likely, mate, he'll meet the rope's end."

Andrew gasped, and slumped. He made immediate moral judgments to himself: *It is wrong and cruel.*

Doyle went on: "We'll know the captain's decision in a few days."

The day of the punishment, the ocean was ruffled with whitecaps and the sky overcast. Whitefish was to meet the rope's end.

The crew gathered on the deck to witness the flogging. Whitefish stood hunch-shouldered next to the rigging, where two burly sailors flanked him. The captain gave the order to strip him to the waist.

His shirt fell to the ground and Whitefish's tattoos stood out against his ashen skin. The sky darkened as the sailors grabbed his hands and tied them to the rigging.

You could hear the crew murmuring, "How many lashes do ya think he'll get?"

The captain yelled, "Lay on twelve lashes with the cat-of-nine-tails."

Andrew started to say something … simultaneously there was a clap of thunder, and Doyle turned to Andrew, saying, "That's about what I expected for a light punishment."

"But … but …"

"But nothing!"

"I don't understand. If he has put us in great danger"— he said, betraying his thoughts—"why the light punishment?"

"Because he's a good worker, the captain don't want to put him out of action for too long."

The ship suddenly rocked, and all hands grabbed onto whatever they could. The burly seaman kicked Whitefish's legs apart so he would stay balanced. Then he vigorously shook the cat-of-nine-tails to separate the knots at the ends of the leather strips that would soon tear at Whitefish's skin.

With the first lash, Whitefish screamed and twisted in pain. Two … three … four. The flogger paused and drew the whip's cords through his fingers to remove the skin and blood. On and on it went, until the tenth lash, when Robert Whitefish collapsed. A nearby sailor threw a pail of water over him. Andrew watched Whitefish's blood tint the water pink. There was no mercy; eleven … twelve … the lashes mangled Robert's flesh. When it was finally over, his mates cut him down and carried him, unconscious, to his bunk.

†††

How could one man have two such separate personalities? Andrew pondered. *On one hand, the Mr. Davis I knew on land was jovial and kind. However, his persona when at sea as Captain Searle is stern and capable of ordering brutal behavior.* Andrew considered that maybe the differences were necessitated by the need to control rough hands.

Ten days later, Doyle and Andrew were ordered to Searle's quarters.

Upon entering the quarters Doyle poked Andrew and whispered, "This has to be something big."

"Why?"

"Notice the gunnery officer and the quartermaster at the table."

Andrew shrugged his shoulders as the captain waved them over.

"Gentlemen, please sit down."

He nodded to Willie, the cabin boy standing in the corner. "Please pour our guests some rum."

"Aye, aye, sir." After pouring the rum, he left quickly.

They sipped their rum.

The captain cleared his throat and said, "Gentlemen, yesterday when I went ashore, I met with some of my informers. They told me that a ship carrying a huge shipment of silver bars ran aground. For safety, the silver was unloaded and stored in the treasury building in Vera Cruz. It's only two blocks from the harbor, and I plan to enter the harbor at night, find the silver, and take it. It shouldn't take but a few hours. Understand this, gentlemen. Everything is dependent on not being spotted when we near Vera Cruz."

Doyle responded, "Captain, the best way is to approach from Guatemala. They will not have the reconnaissance that they would have in the north. However, entering the harbor at night will be tricky. With Andrew's assistance, it can be done."

With a look of shock, Andrew turned his head toward Doyle. "Really? And how can we do that?"

"I know that harbor's approach very well. It will depend on taking fast soundings and calculating the speed of the ship. That I know you can do."

Within days, the ship anchored off the Dutch island of Curacao to obtain fresh provisions. Because Andrew spoke fluent Dutch, he was in charge of the provisioning detail. He was not only a good navigator, but also an outstanding negotiator. He bartered for everything the ship needed, even getting the lowest prices and an extra fifty chickens.

A week later, the *Cagway* anchored off the coast of Guatemala's jungle. This position was far from the known shipping lanes. The thick jungle kept Spanish patrols from spotting the ship.

That night at two bells (1:00 a.m.), the ship raised sail and slowly made its way to Vera Cruz's harbor entrance. Andrew, on the starboard side, threw ahead of the ship, a weighted rope that had knots spaced every six feet. He could calculate the ship's speed by timing the ship as it passed the rope. The amount of water under the ship's hull was calculated by counting the knots. Each knot equalled one fathom.

Andrew called out, "Six fathoms, four knots; five fathoms, four knots."

Mr. Doyle stood alongside the helmsman and directed the ship's course between underwater sandbars and shoals. "Steer port ten points, then starboard five points."

The *Cagway* made its way into the harbor and up to the docks by six bells (3:00 a.m.). The plan was to sneak up behind any guards and cut their throats before they could sound an alarm. Twenty-five men went onshore to steal the silver bars.

Surprisingly, there was only one sleeping guard at the door of the treasury building. The guard didn't have time to flinch before they slit his throat and entered the building. There they found a chest filled with silver bars, which was too heavy to carry. Each man took two bars and headed back to the ship.

A second guard approached and saw the first lying in a pool of blood.

He yelled, "Thieves! We're being robbed!"

Within minutes, several men with swords filled the street. After a short and deadly skirmish, all the Vera Cruz men were dead. The sailors returned to the *Cagway* with the silver bars, and sailed away.

There was jubilation on the *Cagway*, the crew bragging about how they had slaughtered seven men including a very young boy who tried to run away.

While everyone celebrated their good fortune, Andrew lay on his hammock visualising the pillaging and violence that sickened him. He held his hands over his ears to shut out the sounds that tortured his soul.

Chapter 11

1679
The Dinner

Lady Elizabeth continued overseeing all the finances after her husband's death, and the estate flourished. The public perception was that this was due to the guidance of her solicitor and accountants. However, it eventually became known that Lady Elizabeth was *the Lady with a big purse and an even bigger heart.*

One evening, Elizabeth was getting ready for one of her dinner parties to raise money for her favorite charity, A Home for Orphans. Abigail ran into Elizabeth's bedroom, where her handmaid was lacing up her evening gown. Surprised to see her daughter, she pulled away from the maid and ran to Abigail.

She hugged her for a moment, before Abigail squirmed away.

"Mother, I want to go to the party."

"Pet, you're too young."

"I'm not."

"Pet, this is a business party for adults." She kissed Abigail on the forehead, smoothed her hair, and said, "Now go back to your nanny."

The child stomped out, saying, "I'm not too young!"

†††

Dinner was a formal affair in an opulent dining room, the table set to perfection. Crystal glasses sparkled, and servants positioned the gold dinnerware in exactly the proper places, next to the gleaming imported china plates.

The elegant table was set for twenty of Elizabeth's friends, the richest and most important people she knew. Among the assembled were: Col. James Moore; Lord Capel; Sir George, the Teller of Receipts of the Exchequer; Sir George Downing; John Washington and his wife, the half-sister of the Duke of Buckingham; their son, Lawrence; and Sir Edwin, the second Baronet of East Hartley.

Succulent aromas wafted into the dining room. The servants brought in the dinner, which consisted of spiced mussel soup, venison and foie gras terrine, Dover sole, and Cropwell Bishop stilton cheese.

Colonel Moore brought up the topic of the newly created Colonial Office. This office was to dispatch agents to America to enforce the Navigation Acts, which required the legislatures of Virginia and Jamaica to supply permanent tax revenues to England.

Lawrence Washington expressed his belief that land in the Virginia Colony would prove to be an extremely profitable investment.

Sir Edwin's wife, Catharine, sat next to Lady Elizabeth. Catharine, a hefty woman, turned to Lady Elizabeth and, with a booming voice, blared out, "Did you hear the latest news?"

"No," replied Lady Elizabeth.

The guests became quiet and Catharine continued. "My dear, the Duke of Newcastle-upon-Tyne passed away the other day."

Lady Elizabeth responded, "I didn't know he was ill. Was his death expected?"

Catharine said, "I don't know, but since his two sons died in the plague of '66, his title will be vacant and the estates will revert to the Crown."

Some of her guests exclaimed in disbelief, "What a shame!"

Sir Edwin, a string bean of a man with sunken cheeks, banged his hands on the table, saying to his wife, "Not so, my dear! You're not completely accurate."

She glowered, raising her eyebrows, as he continued.

"There was a third male child. However, he died at birth."

A servant standing behind Lady Elizabeth's chair spontaneously said, "No, that's not true." The moment the words rolled off her tongue, the servant put her hands to her mouth. Through her fingers she said, "Oh, I'm sorry, please forgive me, I shouldn't have spoken."

"Mildred, what are you saying?" Lady Elizabeth touched her throat, her eyes widened, and she tilted her head back to look at Mildred.

A hush encompassed the room and everyone stared at Mildred.

She cast her gaze down and said, "I'm so sorry, please forgive me, My Lady, but there exists a third son, born healthy."

Composing herself, Elizabeth asked, "How do you know that?"

Mildred nervously raised her head and wished she had not spoken. However, she went on. "My sister was present when the duchess gave birth. The duchess asked to place her rosary around the child's neck. The duchess died soon after. My sister's friend tried to hand the baby to the duke, but he turned it away, yelling, 'Get that murderer out of my sight. I never want to see it again!' He prostrated himself across his wife's dead body."

Some of the guests gasped, others did not utter a sound. Mildred had paused in her recitation, but Lady Elizabeth insisted she continue.

The servant glanced around uneasily and said, "For days, the only thing my sister spoke about was the infant and what was to become of him. The other servants gossiped extensively and it soon became apparent that the wet nurse, Ranie, was to take him and her own child back to her homeland in Jamaica and raise them both."

Lady Elizabeth's heart leapt in her chest upon hearing the words "baby boy," "Ranie," "Jamaica," and "rosary." She couldn't help but think about Andrew, with a rosary around his neck.

Curious, Lord Capel asked Mildred, "How was she to support herself and the child?"

"The duke promised to send an annual stipend till the baby reached manhood. He also made it very clear that he never wanted to see the child in England again."

"How sad," Sir Edwin remarked.

Lady Elizabeth shuffled her feet under the table, her chin dipped down, and she said, "Thank you, Mildred. You may leave now."

The usually quiet and reserved Sir George of the Exchequer put in his twopence worth. "It's sad for the duke's line and title to die out—the Crown needs all of its supporters at this time. However, without an heir, the duke's estate and entailed property will revert to the Crown."

"Oh!" cried Lady Elizabeth. "As a young girl in Jamaica, I knew a white boy named Andrew, who wore a rosary around his neck. Ranie, a black woman, called him her son."

Sir George went on: "If the boy can be found, however, the title will be intact and he will inherit it all before the exchequer records the transfer and resulting redistribution of said properties." He paused, pulled on his ear, and was about to speak again.

Lady Elizabeth said, "Do you really think it's possible that—"

"I do. I will confirm the veracity of your servant's story."

"How good of you, Sir George," she responded.

"My Lady, those of us who care about the business of the realm, I would hope that any son of the duke would share his ideas and goals for the monarchy."

"Of course, Sir George."

The conversation changed when Sir George Downing bragged about purchasing land at St. James's Park so his residence would be within walking distance of Parliament. He felt he could make a large profit by subdividing the land and building row houses.

Lord Capel asked, "What are you going to call the subdivision?"

Sir George Downing answered smugly, "Downing Street, naturally."

All laughed.

Lady Elizabeth kept mulling over Mildred's statements, and could hardly eat.

†††

Sir George questioned Mildred. She gave him the names of several others who could corroborate her sister's story.

After the conclusion of his investigation, Sir George sent a messenger to Lady Elizabeth, stating that he would like to meet with her at his office as soon as she could.

Early the next morning, the wind howled. The clouds, ominous and pregnant with moisture, didn't deter Elizabeth's feelings of hope. Her coach swayed; the footman's knuckles turned white from holding tight to his seat.

Watching the trees bend and the dirt fly up from the horse's hooves caused Elizabeth's memory to revert to the day when she and Andrew sat on the dock as he pointed out a waterspout in the distance.

The horses neighed and the carriage abruptly stopped under a portico. Lady Elizabeth's thoughts jolted back to the present.

They were now in front of the building of the Teller of Receipts of the Exchequer. The air was still heavy with moisture and sudden bursts of wind made the footman appear clumsy when he struggled to climb down from his high seat. The tails of his jacket flapped wildly as he opened the carriage door. When Lady Elizabeth stepped out, a gust of wind blew her skirt up.

"Oh my," she shrieked, struggling to hold her skirt down.

The wind took her hat. She and the coachman watched it disappear into the ominous gray sky.

A faint smile appeared on her face and she tried to make light of the situation, stating, "At least it's not raining."

Only a few feet away, a guard stood at rigid attention by the door. She scurried over to where he stood.

Trying to be heard over the wind, she yelled, "I'm Lady Elizabeth Loxley. I'm here to see Sir George."

The black plumage on the guard's hat danced in the wind. He barely moved a muscle as he spoke: "Lady Elizabeth, Sir George is expecting you. Go down the corridor, just before the staircase on your right, you'll see his chamber."

He placed his white-gloved hands on the huge door's brass handle and struggled to pull it open against the wind. A loud clap of thunder boomed, and when the door opened, a musty smell hit her nostrils. Lady Elizabeth hurried over the threshold. The clouds erupted.

The long, narrow corridor had sconces gracing the walls; their tapers flickered. Crystal chandeliers pinged and swayed precariously. The beat of her heart accelerated with each step. Her neck muscles tightened in anticipation of the news Sir George would impart. To her right an ornate brass plaque was engraved with Sir George's name.

Her heart galloped as she placed her hand on the wooden doorknob. Sitting behind a high writing desk, engrossed in his task, sat a clerk.

Lady Elizabeth cleared her throat and said, "Excuse me, I am here to see Sir George."

The clerk's head bobbed up, and his small, black, porcupine eyes peered at her through pinched-nose glasses. "Lady Elizabeth, of course. He's expecting you, go right in."

The grandeur of his office didn't surprise her. Sir George arose from behind his baroque carved desk and motioned for her to sit in one of the velvet wing chairs. She fixed her skirts and sat down.

Her insides quivered and her words spilled out: "What have you found?"

Removing his glasses, he placed them on the desk. Sir George smugly smiled and reported: "More than one of the duke's servants has corroborated Mildred's story. I found the doctor in attendance at the birth was Dr. Wallingford. If you want further verification, I suggest that you visit him. Perhaps he kept a record of the event."

Lightheaded and fanning herself with both hands, she asked, "Do you know where Dr. Wallingford resides?"

"Are you all right, Lady Elizabeth?" Sir George asked with great concern.

"Yes, I'm fine." She placed her hands on her lap. "Please tell me where I can find the doctor."

"He's retired, but that shouldn't cause a problem." Sir George smiled and went on. "My clerk, Daryl, can give you his address."

"I appreciate the trouble you've gone to."

"I am as curious as you are." He escorted her to his clerk's desk and instructed Daryl, "Please give Lady Elizabeth the information on Dr. Wallingford."

The clerk handed her a folder that contained the doctor's address.

Sir George interjected, "Oh, I'm getting old. How could I have forgotten?"

"Forgotten what?" she asked.

"In the file you will find that the duke purchased passage on the ship *Jamaica Merchant* for a Mistress Ranie and two infants."

Elizabeth's mind reeled. *Oh my God! It has to be my Andrew.* She shook Sir George's hand—restraining herself from giving him a peck on the cheek—thanked him, and left.

Chapter 12

The Investigation

Lady Elizabeth continued to think about all the ramifications of her servant's information: *If Sir George could find the proper identification, Andrew could accomplish great things because of his compassion, knowledge, and heritage.*

Applying quill to paper, Lady Elizabeth sent a message to Dr. Wallingford, who was now living on the outskirts of London. She explained that she was investigating the birth of a baby boy that the doctor had delivered years ago.

It didn't take long before she received a letter from Dr. Wallingford's daughter, Blyth, explaining that her father was frail but he would see her.

Blyth greeted her warmly and said, "I hope my father can be of assistance to you."

"I'm sure he will," Elizabeth replied.

"He's expecting you. Please follow me."

When they stopped in front of two large French doors, Elizabeth could see the geometric shapes of the bay laurel on either side of a path. Blyth pushed the doors open to let in the sweet smell of lilacs. After walking a few feet through the lush garden, where creeping thyme spread under spikes of lavender, they stopped and Blyth raised her slender hand, pointing to her father.

"Lady Loxley, Father is over there in his chair, beyond the sycamore tree."

Even though it was a warm spring day, Dr. Wallingford sat with a blanket covering his legs.

Approaching with the quietness of a rabbit and being careful not to startle him, Blyth said softly, "Father, Lady Elizabeth is here to speak to you about Lord Loxley."

He stared blankly into space.

Blyth repeated, "Father, Lady Loxley is here. Remember, we spoke about how you might be able to help her?"

Blyth explained to Elizabeth that sometimes he was nonresponsive and she was so sorry that this was one of those times.

Elizabeth extended her hand. "Pleased to meet you, Doctor."

His vacant stare was disquieting. She feared he would not be able to confirm the facts about Andrew's birth.

Hesitantly she asked, "Dr. Wallingford, do you recall the Duchess of Newcastle-upon-Tyne, who gave birth to a son and died soon after?"

Though he was still staring unresponsively, she went on. "Can you tell me anything about the infant? I believe his name was Andrew. Can you assist me in any way?"

There was no reaction.

Lady Elizabeth Loxley looked at Blyth and sighed. "I sincerely hope he gets better."

Blyth nodded. As they started to turn away, Lady Loxley heard a faint sound emanating from the doctor.

She quickly picked up his hand and lightly stroked it. "Please, please tell me what you remember."

A glimmer of light came into the doctor's eyes. Slowly his mouth shaped the words, "Seee Doc ... tor Basss ...."

Then his eyes became rheumy and glazed over. He drifted back into his own world.

Blyth said, "I believe he's trying to say Dr. Bassill. He was his apprentice years ago. The doctor now lives in East London. I can give you his address."

"Please do, he may help me."

A few days later, Lady Elizabeth visited Dr. Bassill's residence. She got right down to business after his housekeeper introduced her to him.

"Dr. Bassill, about twenty-nine years ago, a baby boy was born to the Duke and Duchess of Newcastle-upon-Tyne at their manor. Do you know anything about this?"

"My dear lady, why do you want to know?"

"The duke recently passed away. His sons died in the plague of 1666. Now his title and estates will revert to the Crown if an heir is not found."

Dr. Bassill went over to his desk, removed his glasses, and rubbed the bridge of his nose as he asked her to sit down.

Hesitating, he said, "It was … a very messy affair. … The duke made great efforts to keep the details from public records. You are correct. There is a third son, born on the day the duchess died. However, the duke insisted that we not keep any public record of his birth. How did you come by this knowledge?"

"Sir George of the Exchequer looked into information for me that came to light at a dinner party. The death of the duke was a topic of discussion. The sister of one of my servants was present at the birth twenty-nine years earlier. The result of that conversation was, Sir George and I sought out Dr. Wallingford, who referred me to you."

"Hmm." He nodded and went on. "I recorded the boy's birth in my private journal. I did so to protect Dr. Wallingford and myself in case the duke later had a change of heart or a court battle over an inheritance."

"You've been a great help, Doctor. If necessary, are you willing to produce the record of his birth and give a sworn statement regarding the facts as you know them?"

"Lady Elizabeth, you ask a great deal!"

"Do not concern yourself with anything. I will make it worth your while." Lady Elizabeth removed a five-hundred-pound note from her purse and held it up.

His eyes widened and he said, "That's a year's income!"

"For your trouble, Doctor."

He bowed and said, "Lady Elizabeth, anything you need, I'm at your service."

Chapter 13

The Ring

The seas were smoother than Captain Searle's disposition. The *Cagway* sailed outside of Pensacola in pursuit of treasure. It had been months since their last successful haul.

The lookout shouted from the crow's nest, "Sail away, sail away."

It was music to Captain Searle's ears. He put his glass to his eye and bellowed up to the lookout, "Where away?"

Pointing, the lookout shouted, "There, two points, starboard."

The captain held the glass tightly. He clenched his teeth, and commanded, "Make full sail, helmsman, steer east-southeast."

A whirl of activity began. Men climbed the rigging to unfurl the topsails as others set the jib.

The pursuit was on. It took the *Cagway* only four bells (two hours) to overtake the schooner. When the *Cagway* hoisted the black flag, the schooner's captain surrendered without delay.

After boarding the schooner, the captain and some of his men searched the ship, only to find the hold empty.

Exasperated, the captain ranted and raved. "No treasure. This can't be! There must be something somewhere," the incensed captain yelled.

They forced open cabin doors and found two couples huddled together.

Captain Searle bellowed, "What have we here?"

The women closed their eyes; the men stood stoic with fear. All were barely breathing.

The captain scrutinized them, then demanded, "Hand over your valuables and you'll be spared."

The older man pleaded to his wife and friends, "If we do as he says, we'll be unharmed."

"You listen to him," Captain Searle growled.

The older man dug deep into his pockets, quickly pulled out a few silver coins, and handed them over. Noticing the captain staring at his wife's earrings, he nudged her and touched his earlobe. She understood straightaway, and removed her gold earrings and gave them to the captain.

The younger man fiddled his hand around in his pocket searching for his one coin. Scared and nervous, he held it out, "I'm truly sorry, but that's all I have."

Scowling, the captain's eyes darted at the young woman who clung to the younger man's arm.

"Give me what you have, woman."

Tears ran down her rosy cheeks. "Please, sir, I have nothing, no jewelry or money."

Smoothing out his hair while walking closer to her, he winked, clearing his throat, and said, "Well now, what can you give me?"

She blushed and cast her gaze downward.

The captain snarled, "My, my, you say you have nothing for me?" He snaked around her.

She cringed; his eyes looked her over. She lowered her head and covered her face with her hands. The others watched and listened in frustration.

Coming full circle, he stopped. Picturing her naked, he grinned, and said, "What a lovely body you have, my dear."

She silently prayed, *Please, God, don't let him touch me. I'd rather die.*

"Why do you wear white gloves?" he asked.

She didn't answer.

He ordered, "Bare your hands!"

Her heart pounded and she turned crimson. Ignoring her innermost feelings, she stood her ground in defiance and refused to remove her gloves.

The exasperated captain hollered, "Are you deaf? I said remove your gloves."

"No," she said meekly.

He pointed to his men and ordered, "Remove her gloves!"

One of the sailors grabbed her wrist. She tried to pull her hand back. The younger man started to lunge. Another sailor restrained him as a third sailor pulled off her gloves, revealing a diamond-and-emerald ring.

Infuriated, the captain said, "Your beauty betrays you, my dear. You said you have nothing!" The captain spit on the floor and bellowed, "Take the ring!"

Within minutes, the girl fainted and the confrontation was over.

Staring at her lying on the floor, Captain Searle shouted, "She'll be all right."

Then he and his men reboarded the *Cagway*.

†††

Andrew, standing on the sterncastle, watched five of the crew milling around in a tight circle, and yelled, "What's going on down there?"

One of them looked up. "I'm showing everyone the ring we took from the ship."

"Let me see it."

"Aye, aye."

The men went up to the sterncastle. Andrew's stomach turned when he saw the ring still on a bloody finger. He ran to the rail and threw up. The crew had a good laugh.

From that day forth, Andrew had nightmares of a girl drowning in a sea of blood, holding her hand up with a digit missing, screaming, "Why did you do this to me?"

Chapter 14

Jumping Ship

After several weeks, Captain Searle approached Andrew to say, "Once we are at a safe port, you will take a small party ashore to resupply the ship's stocks."

That moment, Andrew had an epiphany: *This is my chance to get away from this life.*

The *Cagway* sailed around the tip of Florida and up the Gulf Stream, looking for her next victim. North of St. Augustine, Captain Searle spotted a column of smoke at the mouth of a wide river. Dropping the anchor, he ordered Andrew and his men to take a small boat and go ashore to barter with the Timucua Indians for fresh food supplies.

Upon reaching the shore, Andrew got out of the boat. Before the men started to get off the boat, he stretched his hands out and ordered, "Stay with the boat. I'll come back after I see the chief and arrange for the supplies."

"Aye, aye," the crew answered in unison.

Andrew felt a slight relief as he thought, *My plan will now be possible.*

Venturing into the jungle, he was unnerved by the sounds of unseen creatures. Sweat dripped from his face as he kept slapping his body to chase the bugs away. The only pleasurable thing was the scent of exotic flowers. Checking the direction of the sun's shadows, he headed south to find the Timucuan Indian village, near the French Fort Caroline's remains.

He deducted, *If this God-given opportunity works, I'll be free of this ghastly life. I could reach the Bahamas from there or I can make my way to the Dutch island of Saint Martin and go home to Jamaica.*

Andrew was brought back to reality when someone yelled, *"Detener!"* (Halt!)

Two men in red-and-blue Spanish uniforms pushed their way through the thick underbrush.

With muskets pointed at the intruder, Corp. Juan Sanchez barked, "Put your hands up. Who are you and what are you doing here?"

Andrew extended his arms up and spit out, "I'm Andrew Ranson, a cook from a merchant ship, looking to find fresh food."

Corporal Sanchez shouted, "I don't believe you. Who are you?"

"I'm a cook looking to trade for supplies with the Indians." Andrew now wasn't only perspiring from the heat.

"I know you're lying."

"No."

"We've seen the *Cagway*."

"*Cagway*? Never heard—"

"It's your ship."

Andrew's heart hammered as he said, "My ship left me here to find food. They will be back for me in a day or two."

Private Gomez muttered into the corporal's ear, "If we bring him in, we'll get promoted!"

The corporal paused a moment, looked Andrew up and down, and gave the order, "All right, Private, tie his hands."

Andrew stood helpless, looking down the barrel of the musket. Private Gomez grabbed his hands, bound them in front, and tied a short rope to the bindings. Andrew felt like an animal as they pulled him through the forest.

†††

The two Spanish soldiers pushed Andrew into a cell in the partially constructed Castillo in St. Augustine and informed the commander of his capture.

The commander and the governor of Florida agreed that Andrew's story was true. However, they decided to use Andrew as a catalyst for convincing the Crown that they needed to expand the Castillo de San Marcos. This would help defend St. Augustine and the shipping lanes from pirates and the English in the Carolinas.

Verbally abusing Andrew did not coerce him into admitting he was a pirate. The guards tied him over a cannon and whipped him unmercifully.

To put an end to the pain, Andrew finally confessed to being a pirate. The governor sentenced Andrew to a public execution by the garrote.

†††

A hush came over the crowd when an enormous man in a black hood began slowly twisting the garrote's stick that would strangle Andrew. One turn and the rope tightened, two turns, three turns, the rope bit into Andrew's neck and blood trickled from his throat. Andrew struggled to breathe whilst the rope tightened again; four, five, and his eyes began to bulge … six, and the executioner gave the stick one more mighty twist. Andrew's face turned purplish blue. His body slumped, twisted and jerked. Church bells started to toll for Andrew's departed soul. However, on the last twist, the rope snapped in two! Andrew fell forward like a rag doll, gasping for air.

Father Perez de la Mota was stunned. Bible in hand, he raised his arm toward the heavens and cried out, "It's a miracle! This man has been saved by God!"

The crowd gasped in unison. Father Carlos, who had led Andrew to the plaza, thought to himself, *This is proof that there exists a God.*

Governor Cabrera believed it was not an act of God, but an old rotten rope; he wanted to complete the execution. However, the priests knew the Church was the final authority. In the Church's view, God had spared Andrew; therefore the governor must pardon Andrew for his earthly crimes.

During the following Sunday Mass, Father Perez de la Mota affirmed to his congregation: "Every act is caused by God. All authorities must answer to God. It was obvious that Andrew is a devoted Catholic. Otherwise, he wouldn't have requested a rosary moments before his death. Furthermore, if the governor does not give Andrew a pardon,"— from the altar, the priest paused, pointing and shaking a finger at the governor—"the governor will have demonstrated that he's against the Church and *he* must be excommunicated."

The next day, Governor Cabrera summoned a special meeting of the commander of the Castillo, St. Augustine officials, and the most influential citizens to address the Andrew Ranson problem.

The governor read a confidential letter he had received through Father de la Mota, from Andrew Ranson. It in part read: "There's some design corrections that I can make to the Castillo, which would greatly improve its defensive capabilities. If you design the outer walls at a right triangle with a 90 degree base, the slope of the external wall will lessen the impact force of a cannonball; due to an angle it will disperse its energy over a greater surface."

Days of intense debate followed. Finally, they reached a conclusion. Andrew Ranson must be given a limited pardon, with the following provisions:

1. He may communicate by letter to anyone he wishes; however, all letters must be reviewed and approved by the governor or his appointee.

2. He is to have the status of assistant to the chief engineer of the Castillo.

3. He can be used to interrogate English, French, and Dutch prisoners.

4. He is not allowed to travel outside the walls of St. Augustine.

5. He can earn a full pardon if a fine of 40,000 coins in gold is paid.

The governor gave Andrew permission to send a letter to Ranie. His letter traveled through the Dutch colony of Saint Martin, where it was forwarded to Jamaica.

21 December, 1685

Dear Mother,

I am sorry that I have not communicated with you in such a long time. However, as you will read, it's due to matters out of my control.

I was sent to negotiate for supplies with a French-speaking Indian tribe north of the River Mary in Florida. You cannot imagine the shock I had when a Spanish patrol accused me of being a pirate. They took me, at gunpoint, to St. Augustine and tortured me until I falsely confessed to being a member of a pirate crew.

The governor sentenced me to death by the garrote. However, praise God, the executioner's rope broke. The priest declared that I was saved by God, and gave me sanctuary.

I have partial freedom, and can live and work within the walls of St. Augustine. A full pardon will be given when a fine of 40,000 coins in gold is paid.

I have resigned myself to live out my life under these conditions.

I love and miss you with all my heart.

I would like to know how Bett fares. Have you any knowledge of her? Please write and give me any information, no matter how small; memories of my life with you and Bett are all that sustain me now.

I pray that someday in this life or the next we will all be together again.

Your loving son,

Andrew

Chapter 15

The Voyage

Seeking verification that Andrew in fact was the son of the deceased Duke of Newcastle-upon-Tyne, Elizabeth decided to travel to Jamaica to have Ranie confirm it.

In Elizabeth's possession were sworn statements from Dr. Bassill, and Mildred's sister, a servant who had attended the duchess during the birth of the baby. Furthermore, Mildred remembered the baby was named Andrew and given to a wet nurse to raise.

Elizabeth also had an invoice of the *Jamaica Merchant*, showing a passage paid by the duke for a Miss Ranie and two infants. With these statements in hand, Elizabeth went to the person in charge of record keeping for the peerage of Great Britain. She requested that she be given time to locate the heir to the title of the Duke of Newcastle-upon-Tyne, before the title be declared vacant and the estates revert to the Crown.

In order to corroborate all of the above, Elizabeth knew she needed Ranie's testimony of her first-hand knowledge. Only Ranie could state that Andrew had been entrusted to her in 1650 by the duke, with the proviso that she keep the baby out of his sight.

Elizabeth was willing to undertake the risk of a long and dangerous trans-Atlantic crossing to Jamaica, without a guarantee that Ranie would testify.

Elizabeth and her daughter were working on their needlepoint in the sitting room.

She was mentally replaying the time when she and her own mother also did needlepoint in Jamaica and chattered about the day's events. Now it was different. No chatter … just thoughts of her forthcoming trip and worries of how she would tell Abigail.

Leaning over her daughter's work to get her attention, she remarked, "Abigail, your stitches are neat and tidy."

Engrossed in her needlepoint, Abigail nodded.

Elizabeth's stomach felt as if it had butterflies as she said, "Pet, remember when I told you your real father is a farmer in Jamaica?"

Abigail's mind was in a conundrum. *Why is she bringing this up now?* She looked up uneasily, saying, "Yes."

"I found that your father, Andrew, is the only surviving son of a duke who has recently died. Andrew is entitled to his title and estate. Pet, I'm the only one who knows he's the rightful heir and can prove it. I want him to acquire everything he deserves. The only way for me to do that is to travel to Jamaica."

Delighted, Abigail responded, "Oh, Mother, I will love traveling with you."

Quirking an eyebrow and smiling, Elizabeth cleared her throat and said, "No, you don't understand. You cannot come. It's too long of a trip and extremely dangerous!"

Abigail jumped up, placed her hands on her hips, arched her back, stomped her foot, and demanded, "Where you go, I will go!"

Elizabeth reflected to the long-ago confrontation with her own father, when she had stuck her chin out, stiffened her back, placed her hands on her hips, and ranted, "I will not marry Lord Loxley, I love Andrew!"

Now knowing that giving in to her father's wishes had been the biggest mistake she had made in her life, she decided to consider Abigail's demands carefully.

Abigail's voice was strained: "Mother, Mother, I want to meet my real father."

When Elizabeth heard 'meet my real father,' it snapped her out of her trance.

"Pet, I'm not going to insist that you stay. However, you must understand we will endure terrible hardships and we may never see England again. Even worse, we could perish at sea."

Abigail tightened her lips and asserted, "Mother, I understand, but I must go!"

"Are you sure? Take some time to think about it before you give me your final answer. Once we set sail there's no going back."

Abigail reiterated, "I made up my mind. I am going to Jamaica with you."

"Pet, if you feel that strongly …." Elizabeth leaned over, put her arm around her daughter's shoulder, pulled her in gently, and kissed her cheek. … "I'll tell the servants to make ready for the trip."

Abigail's eyes sparkled, her voice bubbled. "Oh, Mother, thank you." Kissing her, she added, "You'll see, I won't be any trouble."

✝✝✝

Lady Elizabeth chartered a Portuguese galleon for themselves and their entourage. The *Padre Etrno* was the largest, most modern ship of its kind. Having heard stories that ships never had enough food or water, she told the captain that she and her people would be self-sufficient and bring all they needed for the voyage.

On the day of departure, a convoy of carriages arrived at the dock, jammed with wardrobes and chests of clothing, crates of dried salted lamb, pork and fish, along with dried peas, beans, and cheese. Not wanting to drink from the ship's communal water supply, they brought barrels of wine and beer.

It wasn't until they were out on the sea that Elizabeth realized the mercenary nature of the captain. The lower decks concealed indentured people of all ages, who were fleeing the misfortune of the old world. They had sold their services, for seven years, to wealthy Virginia colonialists for the price of their passage. Some of them ran up to the open deck to vomit over the rail from the unremitting rocking and pitching of the ship.

Weeks turned into wretched months. People in hidden passages suffered from dysentery, headaches, constipation, infections, and scurvy. They had very little light and air. Rain and seawater seeped through the cracks of the upper decks, keeping them and their belongings wet. One woman went into premature labor. The baby died and was immediately thrown overboard.

The ship's food and water ran out due to the captain's pence-pinching.

After more than two months of endless sea, they hoped this day would be different. Elizabeth and Abigail made their way to the deck to get some fresh air. Abigail grabbed the railing, and Elizabeth held her skirts down as the wind howled and rattled the rigging.

Abigail's grip tightened as she raised her other hand and pointed out to sea, screaming, "Land, Mother, look, land!"

"Take it easy, pet. You'll fall overboard." Elizabeth grabbed her daughter and pulled her back from the rail.

Looking to where her daughter pointed, Elizabeth saw a cloud formation she had once seen a long time ago. Her face paled and she blurted out, "Oh my God, it's a waterspout!"

"Mother, are you feeling all right?"

"Yes."

"What's a waterspout?" Abigail anxiously asked.

Trying to keep her composure, Elizabeth said, "It's a tornado on water. It's dangerous." Putting her arm around Abigail, she said, "We must go to our quarters."

The captain shouted to the crew, "Everyone on deck, make full sail." He turned to the helmsmen and yelled, "Steer north by northeast. We must avoid the storm!"

Chapter 16

Rescue at Sea

Despite the best efforts of the crew to avoid the impending storm, the galleon was overcome. Giant waves rolled the ship, washing the compass overboard. Fear and terror seized the entire crew. The captain sent word that everyone must prepare for the ship going down.

Many of the frightened, hysterical passengers huddled together in Lady Elizabeth and Abigail's quarters.

Clutching her hands, Abigail asked, "Mother, what can we do?"

Elizabeth closed her eyes and started to say the Lord's Prayer. "Our Father, who art in heaven, hallowed be thy …"

The group joined in: "Name. Thy kingdom come, thy will be done on earth as it is in heaven."

As they prayed, the waters calmed and the ship steadied.

Without a compass and in a dense fog, they were hopelessly lost. The ship's food stocks were ruined.

Elizabeth and Abigail discussed the horrific food and water shortage that the other passengers were experiencing. Lady Elizabeth and Abigail offered to share their supplies with all the passengers.

A voice pierced the fog: "Ahoy there, are you in misfortune?"

With renewed hope, the captain turned toward the direction of the voice and made out the faint outline of another ship. "Yes, we don't know our position. We've lost our compass. Can you assist?"

The voice questioned, "Who are you? What is your destination?"

"The Portuguese galleon, *Padre Etrno*, making way to Port Royal."

"I will send a small boat with a compass. You are one hundred leagues southeast of Cuba."

"Thank you for your assistance. Who are you?"

"I'm Captain Searle of the *Cagway*, an English privateer. May God be with you."

A week later, the galleon docked in Port Royal, Jamaica.

Standing on the deck, the captain, crew, and passengers formed a path to the gangplank. When Elizabeth and her daughter appeared from their quarters, the crowd broke out cheering.

Upon approaching the gangplank, the captain bowed and said, "Your Ladyship, the contribution of your supplies saved many lives. God bless you!"

They curtsied.

"We will be eternally grateful for your generosity."

Then he kissed Elizabeth's and Abigail's hands. Embarrassed, Abigail blushed.

The sounds of the cheers changed Abigail's feelings to excitement. She beamed and said, "Mother, you're a hero."

"No, dear, we just did the right thing."

Chapter 17

The Discovery

After securing lodgings, Elizabeth proceeded to search for information regarding the whereabouts of Ranie and Andrew. She learned that Ranie had purchased another farm on Port Royal Street, just outside of Kingston; however, no one had seen Andrew.

Grateful for the news, Elizabeth hired a carriage to take her and her daughter to Ranie's farm. Approaching the farm, they could see the silhouette of a woman sweeping a porch.

"Look, Mother! Is that Ranie?"

Elizabeth clutched her purse tightly and smiled, nodding yes.

Ranie heard the carriage come to a halt and she stopped sweeping. Looking up, she thought, *I don't expect anyone. Who could this be?*

When Elizabeth and Abigail stepped down from the coach, Ranie dropped her broom. *It can't be. Impossible!* She called out, "Is it really you? Is it really you, Elizabeth?"

They ran toward each other and embraced.

Holding Elizabeth out at arm's length, Ranie said, "It's been much too long. I can't believe ..." she paused, looking at Abigail. "And who's this beautiful young lady?"

"My daughter, Abigail." Elizabeth put her arm around Abigail. "My pet, this is Andrew's mother, Ranie."

Abigail curtsied and grinned. "Pleased to make your acquaintance, ma'am."

Ranie's eyes fixated on her. *What good manners,* Ranie thought as she said, "Abigail, it's a pleasure to meet you. Please, both of you do come in, we have a lot of catching up to do."

Elated, they entered the cottage. Ranie pointed to the chairs around the kitchen table, saying, "Please sit. I'll put on the kettle."

After some small talk, Elizabeth stated, "I don't know if you're aware that I married Lord Loxley."

"Oh …." Ranie started to pour the tea as Elizabeth went on. "Through him I became acquainted with the Duke and Duchess of Newcastle-upon-Tyne, and in fact I employed Mildred, the sister of their former servant. From her, I learned the duchess died giving birth to a third son."

Upon hearing this, Ranie spilled the tea. She thought, *Why is she telling me this? Does she know of my connection with the duke?*

Elizabeth said, "Unfortunately, my husband came to an untimely death."

"How sad," Ranie responded.

"In the years following his death, I moved about society more freely and began to entertain. I learned of the death of the Duke of Newcastle-upon-Tyne through a guest at one of my dinners. We discussed the fact that the duke was the end of his line and his title will revert to the Crown, unless he had an heir."

"My goodness …"

Elizabeth continued. "Ranie, I know Andrew is the duke's rightful heir, and I'm hoping you will testify that Andrew is the only surviving son of the duke and duchess."

"I promised the duke I would never reveal Andrew's heritage, not even to Andrew!"

"Ranie, you can't stand in the way of Andrew's inheritance. He's of noble birth and rightfully the new Duke of Newcastle-upon-Tyne."

"Elizabeth, you must give me time to think this over."

"The duke is dead! You are free to reveal all the details involving Andrew's birth."

"Why have you gone to such extents for Andrew?"

"He has been the only one I've ever loved. I have proof of my love for him."

"And what is that?"

Elizabeth looked at Abigail and instructed her to push back her long brown hair, revealing, behind her left ear, a raspberry birthmark.

"See, it's the family birthmark of the Duke of Newcastle-upon-Tyne."

After a beat of strained silence, Ranie gasped, "Abigail is Andrew's child? ... Then she is my granddaughter!"

Turning to Abigail, Ranie said, "Now that I look again, I see the resemblance."

"My mother told me a long time ago that Lord Loxley was not my real father and my nature is that of my true father, Andrew."

Ranie shed tears of joy.

Elizabeth asked, "Where is Andrew?"

Rubbing her hands together, "I don't know how to tell you this ..."

"Tell me what?"

"He's—he's being held captive in St. Augustine, Florida."

Shaken, she said, "Oh my God, is he all right? How do you know this? Does he remain in good health?"

"Andrew sent me a letter that explains everything. I'll show it to you."

Ranie went over to a writing desk and took out a Bible. Holding it close to her heart, she walked over to them. Her eyes welled up as she started to say, "My Andrew ..."

Abigail looked at her mother and raised her shoulders, asking, "What now?"

Softly, Elizabeth asked Ranie, "Are you all right?"

"Yes." Carefully she removed a letter that was pressed between the pages. As she read, tears slid down her face.

They all sobbed as she neared the end of the letter.

Composing herself, Elizabeth asserted, "We have to get him out of there!"

Ranie wiped her tears. "How can we do that? There's not 40,000 gold coins in all of Jamaica!"

Abigail stood up and said, "Mother will find a way."

"Yes, pet, with God's help, we will find a way. There's nothing I would not risk for my Andrew."

Chapter 18

The Grand Plan

Within a week, Elizabeth had devised a plan to free Andrew. Knowing that her friend, Augustine Washington, a bilingual actor, was on tour in Jamaica, she contacted him and explained her scheme. He was to portray a Special Representative of Charles II, king of England. Elizabeth was relieved when he accepted.

Augustine groomed for the part by dressing in a full frockcoat of silk and linen with button-back lapels edged with gold lace. A black wide-brim hat with an ostrich feather that waved in the wind sat upon his head. The ensemble was complete with an elegant black walking stick topped by a silver knob.

Next, she chartered a yacht and had a heavy wooden chest placed aboard. The ruse was ready.

Flying a white flag of truce, the yacht arrived at the St. Augustine inlet. Carl, a crewmember, launched a boat that was to take him and Augustine to the St. Augustine seawall. Neither of them said a word as Augustine tried to help Carl transfer the chest into the boat. Slowly they let go of the chest and watched it drop into the boat with a thud. The boat sank a few inches as the chest settled. Proceeding into the boat, Carl chuckled as Augustine, white knuckled, held on to the sides of the boat.

Though Augustine's face paled, his demeanor epitomized the confidence of an actor as he put on a stoic face while Carl rowed to the Castillo's seawall.

✝✝✝

Weak-kneed, Augustine staggered out of the boat mentally exhausted.

Carl pushed and lugged the chest up to only a few feet from the seawall steps. Annoyed, he burst out, "What the hell is in there?"

Augustine walked over to the chest, raised his cane over it, and hit it with a thud. Boastfully he said, "My man, it contains all the hopes and prayers for a safe conclusion of this venture. Thank you for your help. Now go and wait in the boat."

Several Spanish guards ran out of the Castillo and over the drawbridge, with guns pointed at Augustine.

Before they could utter a word, Augustine drew in a deep breath and pompously stated, "My good men, put your guns aside. Go fetch your governor, and tell him King Charles II of England has sent his representative on a matter of international importance." Flicking his hand, he curtly said, "Now go!"

Two of them ran off to inform Governor Zunica about this strange person. Augustine waited while sitting upon the chest. He silently rehearsed and prayed that the plan would work.

When the governor arrived, Augustine was ready for him.

Taking off his hat and bowing deeply, Augustine said, "I give you my king's greetings and have been instructed to speak only to you and in private. Please tell the guards to put their guns down and step away."

Augustine's appearance and tone of voice invoked confidence. Governor Zunica signaled his men to step back.

100

Augustine motioned for the governor to come closer. Trustingly, he did so.

Augustine leaned forward and whispered, "Your captive, Andrew Ranson, is King Charles's son by his favorite mistress. She will not give the king peace of mind until Andrew is back and safe in England. He has sent 40,000 gold coins for you!"

"No!"

"However, first Andrew must be onboard my ship. Only then can I turn the gold over."

Shocked and in disbelief, Governor Zunica pulled away and responded, "I ... well ... I don't ..."

Augustine's eyes glimmered as he raised his cane, pointing it to the chest beside him, and tapped it on its side. "For simply considering His Majesty's request, I'm to give you this." Smiling, Augustine pulled out a gold coin from his pocket and said, "The chest contains a thousand of these."

Governor Zunica greedily eyed the gold coin. He smirked and signaled for one of his guards to lift the lid. A mass of gold coins shined.

The governor stroked his chin, saying, "I'll consider the matter."

Augustine thrust his walking stick over the top of the chest. "Consider the matter?" he yelled. "Governor, are we in agreement or not?"

After nodding yes, the governor ordered two of his guards to bring Andrew Ranson back.

The guards went to Father Perez de la Mota and told him of the arrival of the mysterious English gentleman. "Father, the governor sent us to bring Andrew Ranson to the seawall immediately, and to assure you that his safety is not in question."

Andrew was having breakfast when Father Perez de la Mota gave him the news. Stunned, he dropped his spoon and thought, *What could they possibly want with me?*

"Do you wish to comply?" asked the Father.

"Do you think it's a wise thing to do?"

"My son, do you have ties to England?"

"No, not that I know of. I have a mother in Jamaica."

"The ways of the Lord are often mysterious, my son. You must do what your heart tells you."

Andrew reflected, *Perhaps this is another sign from God; possibly it's the answer to his test that has dominated my life.* "Father, I will go."

The guards accompanied Andrew to the Castillo's seawall. Surprised to see a well-dressed Englishman conversing with the governor, he didn't know what to think.

Augustine placed his hand on Andrew's shoulder and squeezed it gently in signal as he said, "I'm here at the request of His Majesty and your mother."

Andrew started to reply, "My mo—"

Augustine almost imperceptibly nodded his head, while slowly placing his fingers over his lips before tugging at his beard. Andrew got the message and didn't say another word.

Pointing to the yacht in the distance, Augustine said, "The governor has graciously agreed that you may come with us."

Andrew, Augustine, the governor, and one of the Spanish guards climbed into the awaiting craft. The governor commanded the other guard to take the gold-filled chest to his residence.

Augustine asked, "Are you going to leave the chest with the guard? Do you trust them that much?"

With that comment, the governor changed his mind and redirected the guard to place the chest in the boat. The boat sank even lower into the water. They rowed out to the waiting yacht.

As they approached the yacht, Andrew noticed the outline of a single figure in a long hooded cape standing on top of the sterncastle.

✝✝✝

When the boat pulled alongside the yacht, the officer ordered some of his crew to hang the rope net over the side of the ship.

"Ahoy there," he said. Then he commanded, "Send Andrew Ranson up."

The governor yelled back, "Send my gold down and then I'll send Ranson up."

"No. Tie the boat to the net," the officer answered. "We first need Mr. Ranson safely aboard. Besides, the combined weight may sink your boat."

The governor was reluctant, but complied. Once Andrew was aboard, the governor was told to send Augustine and Carl up to get the remaining 39,000 gold coins. Augustine and Carl climbed up, leaving the governor and the guard alone in the rocking boat.

Andrew watched in bewilderment as the mysterious figure on the sterncastle removed a pistol from under the cape and pointed it down at the governor's head.

Then the officer shouted his demand: "Untie the boat and keep what gold you have, or forfeit your life!"

Governor Zunica felt a sensation of strength increase within his body, his nostrils flaring in protest as the officer signaled him to set sail. He could do nothing with the pistol pointing at him.

After watching them sail away, Andrew, stunned and speechless, turned and stared at the mesmerizing caped figure on the sterncastle. Silently and slowly, the figure climbed down to the main deck. Andrew watched the figure place the pistol on a nearby barrel. Then the figure threw the hooded cape off.

Andrew's mouth dropped open, tears welled in his eyes, and he gasped, "Bett, is it really you?"

She smiled and nodded. They ran to each other and embraced.

Whispering in his ear, she said, "Yes, my love, you were right when you told me, so long ago, 'God meant us to be together. Somehow, someday, it will work out. Never forget that. I will always love you.' "

"I never forgot, Bett. It is the only thing that has kept me going."

Augustine Washington stood by, watching.

"Let me introduce you to an actor friend of mine, Augustine Washington, who played the king's representative who obtained your release."

Shaking hands, Andrew said, "I don't understand how you did this, but thank you."

Before Andrew could utter a word, she said, "Let us go to my cabin."

Bett clasped Andrew's hand and led him away.

Once there, she reminded him of the circumstances of their last meeting, stating she was forced to marry Lord Loxley.

"How could I ever forget that, Bett?"

"Andrew, it has been fifteen years. Have you formed any attachments?"

"No. I could never get over you, my only love."

He put his arms around her, drew her close into a warm embrace, and kissed her deeply.

After their long embrace, Bett sighed and said, "Sweetheart, I must share things with you that you don't know about me."

"I don't need to know anything more than we're together again and that's all I need to know."

Elizabeth, sitting unnaturally still, clasped her hands to her chest and closed her eyes, then hesitantly said, "Listen, my love, I must tell you about my husband, Lord Loxley.

He raped and constantly abused me. One night he came home stumbling and yelling profanities. I awoke upon hearing his rantings and went to the top of the landing, where the smell of cheap perfume wafted up from him. I grabbed hold of the banister, looked down, and saw him swaying on the stairwell. My hatred welled up ..."

All Andrew could think of was, *Did that monster abuse Bett?* He said, "I'll kill him—"

"No, I already did."

"What! How?"

"When I got to the landing, Lord Loxley was halfway up the steps. I told him to be quiet because Abigail was awake. Ignoring me, he pulled himself up farther with his left hand. Now only one step away from me, he drew a pistol from his waist and raged, 'Get closer to the edge of the step and get down on your knees, or I will shoot you right now!' I stepped forward and knelt. Loxley placed his pistol to my head, swayed, and fell backward to his death."

"Bett, my love, it was an accident. You didn't cause his death."

She drew closer to Andrew, gently putting her fingers to his lips, and said, "Shush. Listen. My daughter, Abigail, is not Loxley's child."

"What? Whose daughter is she?"

Bett grinned. "Remember our last night together?"

His face flushed. "Yes."

"My love, she's our child and she takes after you."

"How can you be sure?"

"She has your family birthmark."

He felt weightless. Standing up, he took hold of her hands and pulled her to her feet. He kissed her and whispered, "I'm a father ..." and kissed her again.

"I have more good news." She squeezed his hand. "Love, you're the only heir to one of England's vast fortunes and titles."

"What do you mean?"

"Once we get to London, you will have the title of Duke of Newcastle-upon-Tyne."

"A duke! No, it's not true."

"Yes, my love, it is."

"How do you know this? Can you prove it?"

"It's a long story. The fact is your mother, the duchess, died giving birth to you. Your father, the duke, disavowed you and instructed Ranie, your wet nurse, to raise you in Jamaica and keep your heritage a secret."

"How can you be sure?"

"Because Sir George of the Exchequer and I went to great lengths to verify and document all the facts about your noble birth."

Andrew gasped and sat down on the bed. "It's hard to believe."

"Yes, my love, it's all true. I want the captain to take us to London, so we can present the facts and proofs to the proper authorities. But first, before you are presented at court, we will go to a tailor and purchase the proper dress."

Flinging her arms around his neck, she gave him a kiss.

Elated, Andrew said, "Let's not wait. We can have the captain marry us now."

Bett said, "Oh, Andrew, what a wonderful idea!"

"Splendid, my love."

"We'll need a witness. We should have somebody important to us." She paused a moment, grinned, and said, "How about Augustine?"

"I'll go and ask him."

†††

Augustine was standing on the quarterdeck talking to the head rigger, when Andrew interrupted them. "Excuse me, Augustine. We need a favor of you."

Augustine was stunned. "You need a favor from me! What more can I do for you?"

"Lady Elizabeth and I will be eternally grateful for your outstanding service and the skill with which you performed on our behalf."

Augustine bowed his head and responded, "Thank you."

Andrew said, "The captain will marry us now in his cabin. It's our honor to have you witness the ceremony."

Augustine concurred, professing, "No, it's my honor to be your witness."

After the short service, Captain Cox went over to his desk, where a quill and inkpot sat next to some parchment. He wrote: *On this 17th day of June, 1689, Lady Elizabeth Loxley was joined in matrimony to Andrew Ranson onboard the yacht, Meriweather.* He signed it and handed it to Augustine to witness.

The rest of the afternoon and most of night, Bett and Andrew spent in each other's arms.

Chapter 19

Man-O'-War

Augustine joined Elizabeth and Andrew for lunch in their quarters the next day.

After eating and some small talk, Andrew, with cup in hand, made a toast: "To my new friend. Bett and I want to show our appreciation. Is there anything we can assist you in?"

Augustine stood up, hands to his chest. He gazed at Andrew and spoke plainly as he gave the details of his plight. "Dear friends, there is something you can do. My brother owned a successful plantation in Essington, in the Virginia Colony. However, he passed away last year."

"I'm so sorry."

"Thank you, Andrew. Moreover, my sister-in-law wants to return to England to be with her family. She has proposed a transfer of title to me if I can give her 180 pounds." He hesitated, and then continued. "I have half and I know I can earn the rest over time." He was thinking, *I would rather be in a show than face these realities.*

Elizabeth said, "Are you all right?"

A faint smile came across his face. He nodded yes. "Would it be possible for you to loan me the balance for a period of, say, five years?"

"Where, exactly, is Essington?" Elizabeth questioned.

"In the hill country overlooking the Potomac River. It's about 25,000 front feet of beautiful rolling land running between Dogue and Little Huntington Creeks, that lies directly on the Potomac River. My brother divided it into five farms, planting sixty different crops, and raising sheep, cattle, hogs, and horses."

She said, "It sounds delightful. Is there a reason you can't borrow the balance?"

"Being that I'm an actor, no one believes I would be financially responsible."

She whispered into Andrew's ear, "We should help him!"

Andrew smiled and said, "It would give us pleasure to give you what you need as a gift."

Augustine's heart skipped a beat, and then he placed his hand over his heart. "Oh, I'm overwhelmed! ... Thank you."

"I'll draw up the proper documents. I'll need to know your full name and a description of the property."

"Augustine Washington. Mt. Vernon. It's eight thousand acres in the Virginia Colony."

The captain rapidly knocked on the cabin door and opened it. His voice filled the room: "My Lady, there is a Spanish man-o'-war on our starboard."

For a split second Andrew stopped breathing. "What's happening?"

"She's signaling for us to drop sails and to give you up to them, or they will open fire!"

In disbelief, Andrew ran ahead of the others to the main deck.

Seeing a Spanish forty-gun frigate, Andrew turned to Bett and said, "I don't think there's a way out of this, my love."

Bett's eyes swelled with tears.

"I have no choice. We don't have the means to defend ourselves. For everyone's sake, I must give myself up."

Crying, she said, "I can't let you go! What will Abigail and I do without you?"

"You and Abigail will be fine. Go to Ranie and wait there for me. I promise you I'll find a way to join you."

Turning to the captain, he said, "Signal the frigate to send a boat."

While waiting for the boat, Andrew held Bett close and gave her a kiss that she felt down to her toes.

After another long embrace, he said, "Let's not forget our promise to Augustine."

Bett reassured him she would take care of the matter.

A small boat from the Spanish frigate arrived with guards to escort Andrew back. When Andrew climbed aboard, he was shocked to see Governor Zunica standing on the deck waiting for him.

"Señor Ranson, you English think you are clever, but when your man first requested my presence, I had this frigate stand by outside of the Matanzas Inlet."

†††

Bett cried when Andrew departed. Tearfully turning to the captain, she said, "Captain, before going back to Jamaica, I need to go to the Carolina Colony."

Bett thought, *I must see Gov. James Moore and tell him about Andrew. It's important he knows that the Duke of Newcastle-upon-Tyne is held captive by the Spanish in St. Augustine.*

Chapter 20

Queen Anne's War

Andrew resumed his work and limited freedom in St. Augustine. However, every night, he spent locked in the Castillo's chapel.

The stars sparkled in the crisp cloudless sky on November 8, when Governor Moore laid siege to St. Augustine. He used the excuse of the Queen Anne's War of 1702 to land an English force of five hundred militia and three hundred Yamassee Indians.

The Yamassee quickly burned down the nearby Mission Nombre de Dios, a few hundred yards north of the Castillo, while the English militia bombarded the Spanish fortress from the sand bar that formed the south side of the inlet (Anastasia Island).

Overwhelmed by the fear of the combined invading force, Governor Zunica proclaimed to all prisoners that if they helped defend the city, they would receive a full pardon.

Cannons roared for days. Because of the Castillo's soft coquina walls, cannonballs would just stick in them without causing severe damage.

Andrew told Governor Zunica that he should whitewash over the black cannonballs to match the white limestone outer walls at night, without torch light. Each morning the English thought the walls healed themselves

111

and that God protected the Castillo; this destroyed the English morale.

On the fifty-first day of the siege, Governor Moore, fearing that a Spanish fleet would soon arrive from Havana and cut off his escape route, ordered a withdrawal back to the Carolina Colony.

†††

A month after the English withdrawal, Governor Zunica summoned Andrew to meet him on the Castillo's gun deck.

Andrew approached the governor with trepidation, wondering, *What now?*

The governor said, "Andrew, I promised you freedom in exchange for your service during the English raid."

He handed Andrew a parchment with an official red wax seal. "This is your pardon. You are now a free man." Pointing to the seawall where a boat flying a white banner was tied up, he said, "Now go, your family awaits you."

Holding the pardon up high, Andrew walked out of the Castillo to the boat, where standing on the deck were Ranie, Abigail, and Bett.

GLOSSARY

astrolabe: Predecessor to the sextant.

black flag: Pirate flag.

clouds

cumulus: Clouds with a flat, dark base around 2,000 feet, and rounded, white mountainous outlines to altitudes of 10,000 feet, that appears in a broken mass.

cumulonimbus: Thunderstorm clouds that spread from portions at 5,000 feet to towers rising upward to 50,000 feet.

stratus: Flattened streaks of clouds at altitudes of a few hundred feet, similar to ground fog and producing drizzle.

funnel: Tornadic waterspout.

four bells: Two hours.

glass: Telescope.

gold: Currency in the Spanish colonies. Silver cobs are known as "reales" and gold cobs are known as "gold," with two eight-reale coins (about 27 grams each) equaling one escudo.

keelhauled: Dragged under a ship.

league: In the context of nautical distances, the three-[nautical] mile (5.6 km) distance corresponds to how far an observer of average height can see when standing at sea level. Thus, a ship traveling one "league" has reached what was previously the farthest visible distance on the horizon.

Queen Anne's War (1702–1713): Second in a series of wars fought between Great Britain and France in North

America, for control of the continent. It was contemporaneous with the War of the Spanish Succession in Europe. British military aid to the colonists was devoted mainly to defense of the area around Charleston, South Carolina.

rope's end: Flogging.

sterncastle: Raised part of the upper deck at the stern of a ship, in the rear.

Teller of Receipts of the Exchequer: Treasurer of England.

REFERENCES

Ancestry.com: Ships Dover to Jamaica 1650.

Andrew Ranson: Seventeenth-Century Pirate? Author: J. Leitch Wright Jr., *The Florida Historical Quarterly*, Vol. 39, No. 2 (Oct. 1960), pp. 135–144. Published by the Florida Historical Society.

BBC, Feb. 17, 2011, Lambert, Andrew, "Life in the Royal Navy of the 18th Century." www.bbc.co.uk.

Castillo de San Marcos, St. Augustine, FL.

Early Years, Augustine Washington, www.mtvernon.org/educational-resources.

Encyclopedia Britannica, 11th edition, Cambridge Press. (Public Domain)

euroresidents.com/property/vocab/Spanish_house_types.com

Florida Department of State, Div. of Historical Resources, www.flheritage.com.

Florida Keys National Marine Sanctuary, http://floridiakeys.noaa.gov.

Growing up in England: Experiences of Childhood 1600–1914, Anthony Fletcher, Yale University Press, April 30, 2008.

/history/caribbean_islands/caribbean_islands-growth_and_structure_of_the_economy_2080.html#VIXGy5HweHWqSiug.99

http://www.mongabay.com

Institute of Jamaica, P. R. Collection, Museum of History & Ethnography.

The Knot, www.theknot.com. Wedding Toasts: Traditional and Cultural.

Letters, #1. Governor Francisco Guerra y de la Vega to King Charles II, St. Augustine, Aug. 8, 1668, AGI 54-5-18, Connor Col., Library of Congress. Searles's alias was John Davis. #2. Juan Marques to Charles II, St. Augustine, April 8, 1683.

National Park Service, Timucuan Ecological and Historic Preserve, Florida Fort Caroline, France in North America.

Queen Anne's War (1702–13), www.britannica.com.

Ranker.Com, Buccaneer's: Famous 17th-Century Pirates.

Ross, David, UK travel and heritage – Briton Express, "The London Plague Revisited," 14-7-2011.

Stetson Col. 28. Auto de Zufiga, St. Augustine, Nov. 10, 1702, AGI 58-2-8.

Transcripts: L.C. 14. Joseph Fernandez de Cordova a Ponce de Leon to Charles II, Havana, May 20, 1685, AGI 58-2-6.

UK National Archives, Nottinghamshire Archive.

University of Florida Library, 22. Auto de Ruego y Encargo …, op. cit. 23.

University of Florida Monographs, University of Florida Press/Gainesville, *The Siege of St. Augustine in 1702*, Charles W. Arnade.

Water Depth / Sounding Line: To measure the depth of shallow waters, boatmen used a sounding line containing fathom points, some marked and others in between, called deeps, unmarked but estimated by the user. [8] Water near the coast and not too deep to fathom by a hand sounding line was referred to as in soundings or on soundings. [9] The area offshore beyond the 100-fathom (600 feet) line, too deep to be fathomed by a hand sounding line, was referred to as off soundings.

Wormer School History, Jamaica, BWI.

www.bbc.co.uk/history/historic_figures/charles_ii_king.

www.history.com/topics/america-in-the-british-empire

www.navy.mil/Time as marked by the bells: The use of the bells to mark the time stems from the period when seamen (1) could not afford a personal timepiece (i.e., a watch), and (2) even if they could, they had no idea of how to tell time with such an instrument. The bells mark the hours of the watch in half-hour increments. The seamen would know if it were morning, noon, or night. Each watch is four hours long and the bells are struck thus.

www.streetswing.com, Dance History Archives: Waltz.

Yale University – Sterling Memorial Library, (Admiralty documents), 1664–1680, Tewkesbury, Henry Capel, Lord Capel.

DICTIONARIES

The Bad Speller's Dictionary, by Joseph Krevisky and Jordan L. Linfield, published by Innovation Press Random House, New York, 1967, 1963.

Bartlett's Roget's Thesaurus, Little, Brown and Company, 1996.

The Emotion Thesaurus: A Writer's Guide To Character Expression, Angela Ackerman & Becca Puglish, The Bookshelf Muse, 2012.

Random House Word Menu, by Stephen Glazier, Ballantine Books, New York, 1992.

Webster English Dictionary, published by Metro Books by arrangement with Federal Street Press, a division of Merriam-Webster, 2007.

Webster's Dictionary of Synonyms & Antonyms, created in cooperation with the editors of Merriam-Webster, 2003.

Webster's Universal New Dictionary Unabridged, Barnes & Noble Inc., arrangement with Random House Value Publishing, Inc., 1996 Barnes & Noble.

AUTHORS' NOTE

This is a work of imagination inspired by the life of Andrew Ranson, who in 1684, was sentenced to death for piracy and garroted in St. Augustine, Florida.

It is the result of many hours of intensive research and study of actual people and events. Though the characters of Andrew Ranson and others are real, this novella in every way is a work of fiction.

K. Ross Lee and Betsy S. Lee

ABOUT THE AUTHORS

Betsy S. Lee and K. Ross Lee coauthored *Andrew Ranson: St. Augustine's Pirate*, a medallion-winning historical novel. They also collaborated on writing *Seven Red Knots*, a time-travel mystery also set in historic St. Augustine, Florida. *Seven Red Knots* whisks the reader in and out of adventures in the seventeenth, eighteenth, and twenty-first centuries.

Betsy S. Lee is an award-winning author, illustrator, and photographer. She is a member of the Florida Writers Association, a former member and officer of the National League of American Pen Women (St. Augustine Branch), a past member of the American Library Association, and was a featured author at the Amelia Island Book Festival and a participant at the Florida Heritage Book Festival.

Among her awards and honors, Betsy is most proud of receiving the Florida Writers Association's Royal Palm Literary Award (2007), as well as a tribute from the Florida House of Representatives.

Betsy's works include:
Off the Track
Off the Track Coloring & Activities Book
Historic St. Augustine Activities Book

I'm Smarter Than That
Let's Color & Draw
450th Anniversary Commemorative Historic St. Augustine Activities Book

Watch for Betsy's new book, *Off to Hollywood*.

K. Ross Lee is a former member of a leading stock exchange, and was a real estate developer and broker. After retiring he received certification from the U.S. Department of the Interior for the Castillo de San Marcos, as a national monument tour guide as well as for the city of St. Augustine, Florida.

He attended private schools. After rigorous studies for his bar mitzvah, he developed the fervor to search for the lifelong effects of religion on history, as revealed in his books. He has written educational monologues for historical characters, several one-act plays, and routines for stand-up comedians including a magic comedy team. He also founded and was a service leader for a Reform Jewish congregation.

51589274R00073

Made in the USA
Charleston, SC
28 January 2016